To the Dragon Master Reading This Book,

Griffith, the Royal Wizard of Bracken, is a dear friend of mine. We were having tea (that he made appear by magic) and talking about dragons, of course. Griffith was telling me about all the new dragons his Dragon Masters had encountered recently. But he said that he had no time to write down the information he was learning.

"I can help you!" I offered, because I am a writer. (As you may know, I tell the tales of the Dragon Masters' adventures.) I suggested that we make a guidebook, and Griffith liked that idea very much.

We put our heads together and began to create a guidebook — an EPIC guidebook — to help Dragon Masters around the world. In these pages, you will find facts and secrets about Dragon Masters and dragons. You will learn about wizards, magical creatures, and fantastic places.

We hope that by reading this book, *you* will become an even better Dragon Master.

Yours in dragons,

Tracey of the West

THE KINGDOM OF BRACKEN

Bracken is one kingdom in the larger land known as Albion.

Old Oak Woods

Farmers' Village

Farming Fields

Market Square

Valley of Clouds

Hedgehog Hill

Bracken Castle

Otter River

Crafters' Village

3

KING ROLAND AND QUEEN ROSE

King Roland and Queen Rose rule two kingdoms together — Bracken and Arkwood.

King Roland the Bold has been interested in dragons since he was a young man. After becoming king at age twenty-two, he began his search for dragons. He even thought about creating a dragon army to protect his kingdom.

Queen Rose the Just is very interested in the well-being of the dragons. She encourages the king to take good care of them. Many believe she is the reason he gave up his plans for a dragon army!

KING ROLAND'S QUEST FOR DRAGONS

At just fourteen years old, Roland fought in a fierce battle to protect Bracken Castle. The castle was saved, but Roland lost his grandfather, King Harold, in the fight.

When King Roland took the throne, he worried that other kingdoms might attack the land. He knew that Bracken's army might not be large enough to keep enemies at bay. Then he had an idea: What if dragons could protect the kingdom? He asked Griffith to help him learn about dragons around the world.

The king sent soldiers out to capture all kinds of dragons. Griffith thought it was cruel to take the dragons from their homes. The dragons were sometimes wild and upset when they were brought to the castle, but Griffith couldn't communicate with them. He knew that he needed to find Dragon Masters for the dragons right away!

BRACKEN CASTLE

King Harold used the underground floor of the castle as a dungeon, but King Roland turned it into a place where Dragon Masters can work with their dragons.

1 Chapel

2 Castle Staff's Dining Room

3 Kitchen Staff's Chambers

4 Kitchen

5 Larder
(Where food is stored)

6 Dragon Undercroft

7 Griffith's Chambers

8 Dragon Masters' Chambers

9 Dragon Masters' Dining Room

10 King and Queen's Chambers

11 Queen's Dressing Room

12 Nursery
(Where royal
babies are raised)

13 Balcony

14 Banquet Hall

15 Throne Room

16 Lookout Tower

17 Armory
(Where weapons are stored)

18 Guards' Chambers

19 Portrait Gallery

20 Royal Library

21 Music Room

22 Servants' Dining Room

23 Servants' Chambers

THE DRAGON UNDERCROFT

Classroom

This is where Dragon Masters learn their lessons. It holds bookshelves filled with books about dragons.

Training Room
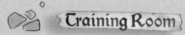

This is where King Roland's Dragon Masters begin their training. The dragons can practice using their powers on command in this safe, indoor space.

Griffith's Workshop

This room contains potions, herbs, and other items used for spells. Griffith's Dragon Stone is here, as well as other magical objects and tools.

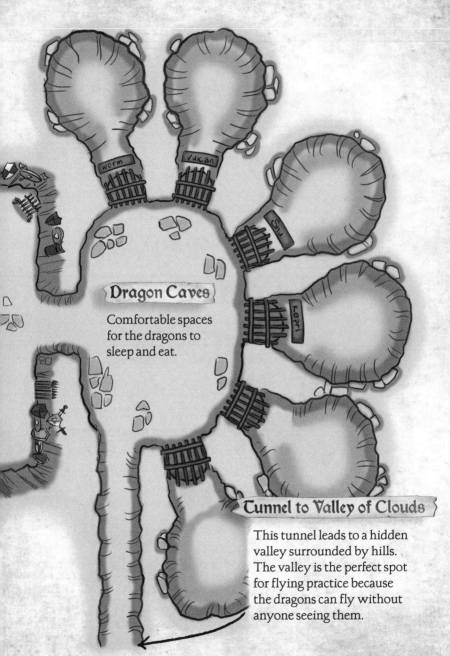

Dragon Caves

Comfortable spaces for the dragons to sleep and eat.

Tunnel to Valley of Clouds

This tunnel leads to a hidden valley surrounded by hills. The valley is the perfect spot for flying practice because the dragons can fly without anyone seeing them.

Wizard

GRIFFITH OF THE GREEN FIELDS

MAGIC LEVEL

47 Nobody is sure what the highest magic level is. Magnus of the High Mountains says he can do Level 100 spells, but nobody has ever seen him do one.

COLOR OF MAGIC

POWERS

Griffith is best at magical spells that use potions or rhymes. He can also perform magic simply by pointing his finger. He can transform things, move things, and make force fields.

BACKGROUND

Griffith grew up in the land of Greenshire, and his parents were farmers. Griffith learned he was a wizard at the age of five. He pointed at a bowl of mushy porridge and transformed it into an apple cake, and his parents sent him to live at the Castle of the Wizards in Belerion. He studied and grew up there.

At eighteen, Griffith found a position as the royal wizard for King Harold of Bracken. For many years, he performed simple tricks to amuse the king and his guests. Then Harold's grandson, King Roland, took the throne. That is when Griffith began to study dragons.

Griffith's Dragon Studies

To study dragons, Griffith set off on a journey that lasted for three years. He spent the first year reading everything he could about dragons in the Great Library of Helas. Then he searched for dragons he could study more easily than the elusive Moss Dragons in Belerion. In Gallia, he managed to track down a Dragon Mage named Marianne who worked with a flock of Mushroom Dragons. Deep in the woods, he closely observed dragon behavior for the first time.

Every wizard takes a name from the land of their birth. I am named for the green fields of my homeland.

-Griffith

GRIFFITH'S WORKSHOP

A workshop is a place to think, to learn, and to create magic spells and potions. Griffith's workshop is on the bottom level in Bracken Castle.

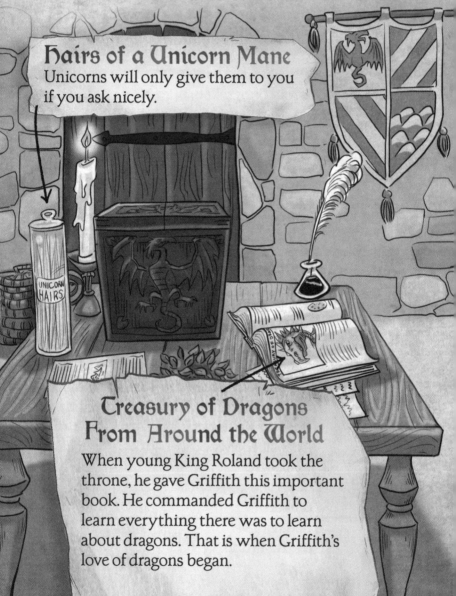

Hairs of a Unicorn Mane
Unicorns will only give them to you if you ask nicely.

Treasury of Dragons From Around the World
When young King Roland took the throne, he gave Griffith this important book. He commanded Griffith to learn everything there was to learn about dragons. That is when Griffith's love of dragons began.

Griffith uses herbs to make all sorts of potions. He gets many of the herbs from Bracken. His wizard friends send him some, too.

Out of Sight
Three drops of this will turn you invisible for one hour.

Condor Feathers
Perfect for flight potions.

Here is lavender from my garden!
—Diego

Moonbeams
These can strengthen spells, but they are difficult to catch.

MAGICAL TOOLS

Wizards can create magic just by pointing a finger. But they make and charm tools, too, for themselves and others. Magical tools often help wizards cast spells and perform tasks more easily.

Magic Mirror

If you and your friend each have a magic mirror, you can talk to each other — no matter how far apart you are! Some wizards can use magic mirrors to send small objects to each other.

Feather of Finding

The feather of this green swallow can be charmed to help you find something that is lost. Ask the feather to lead you to the object, and then follow it!

Spell Book

Each wizard has their own, unique book. They write down the ingredients and magic words for spells they have learned. A spell book can be charged under the full moon to make the spells inside it more powerful.

Gazing Ball

This magical glass ball allows wizards to see what is happening in other places in the world. Very powerful wizards can use them to see the past and the future.

Wand

Every wizard learns how to cast spells by using a wand made from an ash tree or oak tree. As their powers get stronger, most wizards can create magic without using their wands.

MAGICAL OBJECTS

Magical objects are one-of-a-kind items that contain great power. Some of them can be dangerous if they're in the wrong hands!

Silver Sword

This sword is connected to the powers of Argent, the Silver Dragon. The sword can create a portal that takes you to Argent or to where the Silver Dragon has just been.

A portal is a magical doorway from one place to another.

-Griffith

Power Crystal

This crystal absorbs the magic of any wizard who touches it. This powerful gem contains all the magic it has absorbed.

Gold Disc

When you hold the disc in your hand and imagine an object, the gold disc will transform into it.

Tenebrex Stone

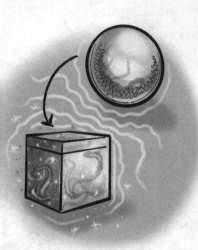

This stone has the power to reverse the dangerous False Life spell. Three dragons — a Sea Dragon, a Lava Dragon, and a Wind Dragon — are needed to make the stone's magic work. The stone will transform into a box. Open it to break the spell!

Star Flute

Legend says the flute was created by Harmonia, the ancient goddess of music. This flute has the power to summon a Star Dragon down from the cosmos.

MAGICAL PLANTS

Magical plants are plants that naturally have magical properties. Wizards use all kinds of magical plants to craft spells, but you don't need to be a wizard for magical plants to affect you. Many folks have had unlucky encounters with plants such as these.

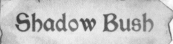

Shadow Bush

If you prick your finger with the thorn of a shadow bush, you will turn into a shadow. That's a useful trick if you need to sneak into a place or spy on someone. However, you must prick yourself a second time within the hour, or you'll stay a shadow forever.

Five-Petal Fairy Flower

Drake found these in the magical fairy world of Inis Banba. When sprinkled with fairy dust, they grow large enough to swallow a human.

I hope to spend more time with Vanad, a wizard from Sindhu. He is an expert on magical plants from around the world.

-Griffith

Moonberry Tree

There is only one moonberry tree.
It is found deep in the Dark Forest
at the base of the Lofty Mountains.
White berries grow on it. Anyone
who eats a berry — just one — will
turn into a furry monster when the
moon is full.

Dragon Flower

This flower was created by Fallyn
the Spring Dragon, and it looks
like a dragon breathing fire. Plant
experts in Belerion are testing it to
see if it has magical properties.

Magical Rocks and Gems

Like flowers, some rocks and gems naturally
have magical powers, too. For example,
wearing a Star Ruby can give you the power of
flight. However, it's impossible to tell when the
magic will wear off. And crystals with many
different magical powers grow in a cave in
Cambria.

THE PRIME STONE

Almost every Dragon Stone comes from one very big, very old stone: the prime stone. It is hidden inside the Pyramid of the Seven Dragons, in the Land of Pyramids.

Every ten thousand years, energy from the prime stone creates a Lightning Dragon egg. The stone feeds energy to the egg, so its powers are weakened until the egg hatches.

Nobody is sure how old the prime stone is, or where it came from. Is it a wonder of nature? Was it created by powerful wizards, or some other kind of magic? There  may be more secrets to be discovered inside that pyramid.

DRAGON STONES

Dragon Masters and wizards both use Dragon Stones, but in different ways.

Dragon Masters

Every Dragon Master wears a small piece of the Dragon Stone. At first, the Dragon Master can give the dragon simple commands. When their bond grows strong, and they can reach each other's minds, the stone will glow green. This connection becomes even stronger as the Dragon Master and dragon work together.

Wizards

If a wizard wants to train a Dragon Master, he or she must first find a Dragon Stone. Wizards ask their Dragon Stone to choose a Dragon Master to match with a dragon. An image of the Dragon Master will appear inside a green beam of light given off by the stone.

OTHER DRAGON STONES

Ahi Stone

This green stone comes from the heart of a volcano. Dragon Masters Opeli and Manawa live on islands with volcanoes. They both use Ahi Stones to communicate with their dragons. Ahi Stones seem to work exactly the same as Dragon Stones. Nobody knows for sure the connection between Ahi Stones and the prime stone. But Drake once guessed that the prime stone might have come from a volcano.

Red Dragon Stone

Evil wizard magic creates this type of stone. A wizard can use a red Dragon Stone to make any dragon follow orders. Maldred used one to control Zera and then Worm. Gerik used one to control Belydor. Thankfully, this stone is easy to break; and once broken, its magic is broken, too.

The Secret of Green Lake

Getting my Dragon Stone was not easy. I knew that wizards in the Far North Lands had been using these stones for many years. So I asked my wizard friend Hulda where to find one. She told me that a piece of the prime stone might be found in the bottom of a magical body of water known as Green Lake.

I traveled far to reach the lake. Once I got there, I dove to the very bottom. I found my Dragon Stone and brought it back to Bracken. Then I used it to find Dragon Masters for King Roland's dragons.

-Griffith

A HISTORY OF DRAGON MASTERS

These four Dragon Masters are some of the most famous in history.

Ancient scrolls say that the first Dragon Master was Ast, from the Land of Pyramids. She was chosen by the prime Dragon Stone more than two thousand years ago.

Ast

Justina

Five hundred years later, a Dragon Master named Justina from Byzantia fought for the safety of dragons. She rescued and took care of dragons that had been captured and mistreated.

This Dragon Master is remembered for his beautiful poetry about dragons. Blind since birth, Jia lived one thousand years ago in the Land of the Far East.

Jia

Borg

This young Dragon Master is famous in tales from the Land of the Far North. Six hundred years ago, Borg and his Ice Dragon, Halvor, defended their village from an attack by sea. Halvor froze the water with his icy breath!

Rules of the Stone

- The Dragon Stone almost always chooses a Dragon Master who is eight years old. Some experts think this might be the best age for a human and dragon to make a connection. The hearts and minds of children this age are open to new ideas.

- A Dragon Master will always keep the connection to their dragon. But if a Dragon Master needs to give up that connection for any reason, a new Dragon Master can be chosen.

Dragon Masters come from all over the world, and they are all different. Not all can see, or hear, or walk. But all Dragon Masters have good hearts.

-Griffith

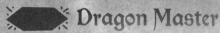 Dragon Master

DRAKE GEORGE

HOME

Drake was born in the Kingdom of Bracken. He lives there still, now in King Roland's castle.

Shadow Drake

Drake once bravely turned himself into a shadow using a shadow thorn. Luckily, he did not stay a shadow forever!

STRENGTHS

Drake is friendly and eager to learn new things. He will always do what is needed to save the day. When he first came to the castle, he didn't feel like he belonged. But thanks to his friendship with Bo, and connection to Worm, he gained confidence.

Drake comes from a family of expert onion growers in Bracken's Farmers' Village. He worked in the fields with his mother, Matilda, and his five older brothers: Arthur, Byron, Clinton, Darren, and Kelvin.

DRAGON

Worm the Earth Dragon

DRAKE'S TIPS FOR DRAGON CARE

Depending upon the type of dragon you have, your dragon might need special care. But every dragon needs three basic things: food, shelter, and a good scale scrubbing now and then.

Feeding Your Dragon

Earth Dragons like my dragon, Worm, prefer veggies that grow in the ground. Carrots and potatoes are his favorite. Fire Dragons love spicy food, like peppers. Water Dragons dine on fish. Your dragon will let you know his or her favorite food when you connect.

Dragons do not need to eat every day. But after they use their powers, they are extra hungry!

Training Tip

Feeding your dragon a treat will put him in a good mood before a training session. Worm loves apples!

Your Dragon's Nest

Dragons need their own area where they can sleep and rest. Make sure that your dragon has enough space to move around in. Add plenty of hay to make a nice, soft bed. My friend Carlos made a nest for his Lightning Dragon, Lalo, and his dragon loves it!

Shining Dragon Scales

Not all dragons' scales are shiny. But all dragons like to have their scales brushed and cleaned. Especially Worm!

THE FARMERS' VILLAGE

Most people who live in the Kingdom of Bracken are farmers. Family members work together to grow vegetables: oats, barley, beans, peas, wheat, potatoes, cabbages, parsnips, carrots, spinach, or onions.

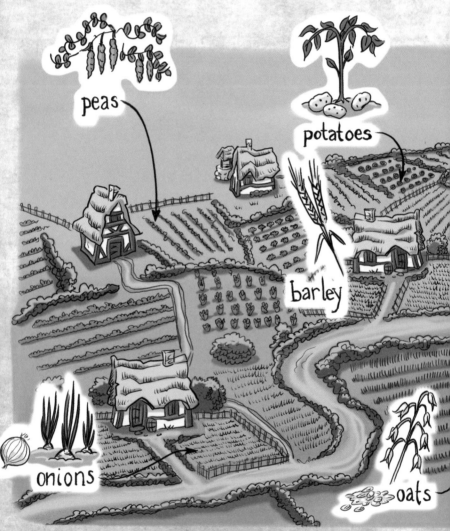

peas

potatoes

barley

onions

oats

Each family gives part of the harvest to King Roland to feed the residents of the castle. The farmers are free to eat, trade, or sell the rest in the market.

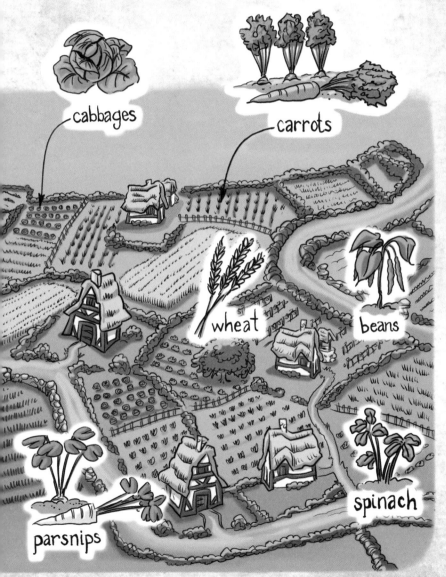

cabbages

carrots

wheat

beans

parsnips

spinach

Dragon
WORM THE
EARTH DRAGON

Worm is an amazing dragon.
The powers of his mind can do almost
anything!

DRAGON MASTER

Drake George

- Worm can instantly transport to any place in the world.

- He can move things with his mind. He can break apart rocks and walls.

- He can use his energy to create a protective shield.

- He can often sense when danger is coming. Worm also knows when a living thing is near, but can't be seen.

- He can shoot energy beams from his eyes to blast things.

- He can use his energy to stop things from moving and he can create green bubbles that capture things in midair.

- Worm can connect with rocks deep inside the ground and make them rise to the surface.

POWER COLOR

SIZE

LENGTH: 42 feet

WEIGHT: 7,100 pounds

EARTH DRAGONS

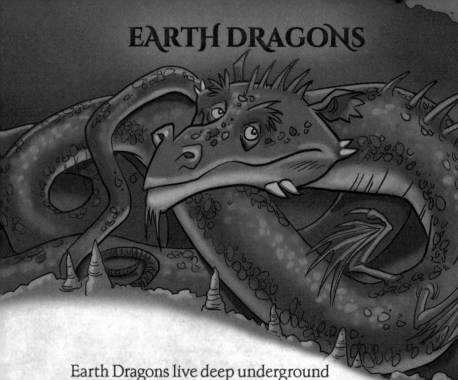

Earth Dragons live deep underground in tunnels and very rarely come to the surface. While most other dragons live alone, Earth Dragons prefer to live together. Explorers have found as many as twelve in one place.

All Earth Dragons have very strong mind powers. Why, then, do they live hidden away? No one knows for sure. But it may be because they are peaceful creatures who simply enjoy one another's company.

Some dragon experts believe that Earth Dragons are related to the Naga, a legendary Earthquake Dragon. Earth Dragons and the Naga have similar powers. Earth Dragons can move things with their minds. The Naga can make the earth shake just by thinking about it.

The Naga

I wonder if Earth Dragons are related to Time Dragons. Earth Dragons can transport to any place. Time Dragons can transport to any place and time. There is a Time Dragon in Casgore I would like to meet...

-Griffith

RORI SMITH

HOME

Rori was born in the Kingdom of Bracken. She lives there still, now in King Roland's castle.

STRENGTHS

Rori is very brave, and she is a good problem solver. She is not afraid to fight for what she believes in. She has a strong will, which sometimes means she doesn't like to follow orders. And while she likes to argue with people, she rarely argues with her best friend, Ana.

Key to the Castle

The key Rori swiped from one of the castle guards isn't magic, but it is pretty close. She can use it to open any lock in the castle.

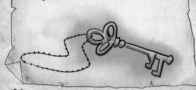

Before becoming a Dragon Master, Rori lived with her mother, Dorothy, her father, William, and her two sisters, Grace and Emma. William is a blacksmith.

DRAGON

Vulcan the Fire Dragon

RORI'S TEAMWORK TIPS

When I told Griffith I wanted to write about teamwork for this epic guidebook, he looked at me funny. "Rori, you have not always been good at working on a team," he said. But I told him that's exactly why I should be the one to write about this! Because I'm getting better at it, and I know how to explain it.

Listen to Your Friends

When you're planning a mission, you might think your idea is the best. (My ideas usually are!) But I learned that sometimes, other people have better ideas. Or, we can combine all of our ideas to make a really great new idea! So, remember to listen to your friends.

Stick with Your Friends

Sometimes I do things on my own and forget that I have friends to help me. One time, I flew on Vulcan to battle Maldred all by myself. Eko says that was brave but foolish. I could have gotten hurt. Now I try to remember that our team is stronger when we work together. Like when Petra and Darpan teamed up to help summon the Star Dragon.

Be Kind to Your Friends

My best friend, Ana, is super nice all the time. I am not. Sometimes I say things without thinking first. Teams work better when everyone gets along. I try really hard to be thoughtful about what I say now. Ana says I'm doing a great job!

THE CRAFTERS' VILLAGE

All of the makers in the Kingdom of Bracken live and work in this village. Rori's family lives here.

Carpenter's Shop

If you need a chair or a table, this is where to go.

This is where I bought the carved box that holds the Dragon Stone.

—Griffith

Bows and Arrows

These weapons can be used for hunting—or for defending the kingdom.

Tailor's Shop

The workers in this shop make fine clothes.

Bakery

The baker provides the castle with one hundred loaves of bread every morning. Villagers can buy bread here or use the ovens to bake their own bread for a penny.

Blacksmith's Shop

William Smith, Rori's father, works here. He makes tools for farming, and his horseshoes are excellent.

Bucket Shop

Wooden buckets are the best—and only—way to carry water from a well.

Dragon
VULCAN THE FIRE DRAGON

Vulcan's fire blasts are very powerful, but he sometimes has a hard time controlling them.

DRAGON MASTER

Rori Smith

POWERS

- Vulcan can shoot fireballs from his mouth.

- He can shoot streams of fire from his nose.

- He can fly.

POWER COLOR

When Vulcan is happy, he will sometimes shoot sparks out of his nose! But don't get too close to him when he does this. I once lost my beard after Rori told him a joke!
-Griffith

SIZE

LENGTH: 20 feet
WEIGHT: 6,800 pounds

Training Tip

Target practice is very helpful for Vulcan to learn how to control his powers. But it's always good to have a Water Dragon nearby!

FIRE DRAGONS

Fire Dragons are found all over the Middle Lands. There are tales of them from Albion, Gallia, Casgore, Kinland, and Remus. Fire Dragons live alone in caves.

People fear Fire Dragons, because their fire powers can be so destructive. But when paired with a Dragon Master, a Fire Dragon can be quite useful.

There is still much to be learned about how to control a Fire Dragon's wild powers. A wizard named Shula is trying to find out where their power comes from. She believes that Fire Dragons may have an inner chamber of fuel inside their bellies.

Fire Dragons may be related to Lava Dragons, who get their fiery power from volcanoes. Fire Dragons shoot fire, while Lava Dragons shoot hot lava.

-Griffith

Wizard
MALDRED OF THE RED HILLS

MAGIC LEVEL

It has never been tested, but his level is at least a 71.

COLOR OF MAGIC

POWERS

Maldred can do many things with his evil powers. He can freeze or zap his opponents with a blast of red energy. He can cast spells to make them obey him. His red magic bubbles can trap opponents. A sprinkle of his red magic dust can transport people or objects a short distance. He creates magical orbs that he can send to a place far away. And once, he created a red Dragon Stone that he used to control a dragon!

Maldred grew up in the harsh lands of Redbern. Life is not easy there. Nothing much grows in this rocky, dry land.

When Maldred discovered that he could do magic, he did not go to the Castle of the Wizards. Nobody in his land knew about wizards, so they were afraid of him and his powers. He was sent away from his village.

In order to survive on his own, Maldred was forced to use his magic. For this reason, his magic became very strong. But because he had no teachers, there was nobody to guide him or to warn him about the dangerous pull of evil magic.

He is one of the most powerful wizards the world has ever seen. But the last time Maldred tried to destroy the world, Griffith transformed him into a horde of buzzing flies.

Red Alert

A wizard's magical energy can be any color. But wizards who use evil magic, like Maldred, always seem to have red energy.

MALDRED'S WORKSHOP

Maldred's workshop is located in a magical dimension. Drake, Rori, and Darma found it using the energy from a portal. Like other wizard workshops, it contains books, potions, and magical ingredients.

The workshop is in a large tower with a spiral staircase.

Evil Spells
Maldred's books are mostly spells for evil magic.

Magic Eye
Maldred uses this to hypnotize anyone who stands in front of it.

Wall of Wizards

Many wizards, good and evil, have challenged Maldred in battle. When they lost, he trapped them in time, inside a magical wall in his workshop.

Journals

He keeps a record of all of his magical battles.

Red Magic

This potion is the main ingredient in Maldred's red magical orbs.

Dragon Master
BO YIN

HOME

Bo grew up in the Kingdom of Caves. He currently lives in Bracken castle.

Bo's Silver Shield

Jean Arcand, the Dragon Master of the Silver Dragon, gave Bo this special shield. It is much stronger than an ordinary shield.

STRENGTHS

Bo stays calm when things go wrong. He is sensitive to the feelings of others and was very kind to Drake when Drake first came to Bracken Castle.

BACKGROUND

Back home, Bo lived with his mother, Fan, and his father, Renshu. He has two younger sisters, Dandan and Jun, and two younger brothers, Heng and Li.

DRAGON

Shu the Water Dragon

BO'S TIPS FOR DRAGON CONNECTION

As a new Dragon Master, your first goal will be to connect with your dragon. For some, this happens quickly. For others, it takes time. Do not worry about how long it takes. The most important thing is to make a strong bond with your dragon. I hope my tips will help!

Always Be Kind

Be kind to your dragon. Feed them a favorite treat. Be gentle with them. Speak to them in a calm voice and never, ever yell. You would not bond with a person who treated you badly, would you? Your dragon needs to know they can trust you.

Have Fun Together!

Training your dragon is important. But if all you do is train, you will never bond. Spend time getting to know your dragon. Read your dragon a story. Go outside and relax together in the sunshine. Shu especially likes when we go for a swim!

Open Your Heart

I know some Dragon Masters who could not connect with their dragons because they were not ready yet. Petra was afraid of her dragon, Zera. Oskar doubted that a tiny dragon like Wildroot could be a great and powerful dragon. But when Petra and Oskar opened their hearts, they saw the best in their dragons. Remember, the Dragon Stone has chosen you for a reason! Trust that you and your dragon were meant to be together.

THE KINGDOM OF CAVES

Far to the east of Bracken, where the land touches the Great Blue Sea, sits the Kingdom of Caves. Many caves can be found along the seaside, and Water Dragons are often found in them.

This kingdom is also known for its talented artists and musicians. In the royal city, you will find many sculptures and paintings of dragons.

Emperor Song's Palace

Water Dragon Caves

Great Blue Sea

Emperor Song

Emperor Song rules a large kingdom in the Land of the Far East. The emperor is fond of dragons. Images of dragons decorate his palace.

He is a fair ruler who allowed Bo to leave the kingdom and go to Bracken at King Roland's request.

The Raven Guard

A group of skilled fighters that serves the emperor. They dress all in black and can move silently without being seen. They are excellent spies.

Dragon
SHU THE
WATER DRAGON

Shu's water powers can
have the strength of a
tidal wave. But she has
a gentle spirit.

DRAGON MASTER

Bo Yin

POWERS

- Shu can fly by floating on air currents (just like a boat floats on ocean waves).

- She can shoot streams of water from her mouth.

- She can create great waves using nearby bodies of water.

- She can breathe out a blue mist that can wash away any spell.

POWER COLOR

SIZE

LENGTH: 17 feet

WEIGHT: 2,900 pounds

Training Tip

Shu practices controlling her water powers by aiming blasts at targets.

57

WATER DRAGONS

Water Dragons, like Shu, are born in caves in the Land of the Far East. They spend much of their days in the water, and sleep in their caves at night.

In different parts of the world, you may find dragons called Lake Dragons, Pond Dragons, Sea Dragons, or more. They may look different than Shu, but they all have one thing in common: They get their powers from the energy of water.

Water Dragons can have many powers: water powers, the power of flight, and special healing powers.

A Sea Dragon named Tani lives on the island of Kapua. Tani is twice as big as Shu and very powerful. I would love to study the two dragons side by side to learn more about what makes them each unique.

-Griffith

Dragon Master

ANA GAMAL

HOME

Ana grew up in the Land of Pyramids. She currently lives in Bracken castle.

STRENGTHS

Ana has a positive, sunny personality. She is clever and is always figuring out new ways to use her dragon's powers. Ana is a good friend to all of the Dragon Masters who live in the castle.

Ana lost her mother when she was a baby. Her father, Abrax, is a traveling merchant who sells beautiful fabrics. Growing up, Ana went with him on trips to faraway lands. She has seen more places in the world than many of the other Dragon Masters.

DRAGON

Kepri the Sun Dragon

ANA'S TIPS FOR MEETING PEOPLE

I love meeting new people, don't you? When you are a Dragon Master, you will travel to many different lands. Some people will be happy to see you. Some people might be afraid of you and your dragon. Others might even seem angry! Don't worry. These tips should help things go smoothly whenever you meet someone new.

Introduce Yourself

Don't wait for someone to ask, "Who are you?" Start by saying your name. Then say something to put people at ease, such as, "I am friendly! My dragon and I are not here to hurt you." This helps calm people who think you or your dragon might want to harm them.

Ask Questions

Asking questions can be a great way to get to know someone better. You might learn that you two have something in common. I like finding out about where a new friend grew up. And it's fun to ask Dragon Masters how they first connected with their dragons.

Offer to Help

Some people won't tell you when they need help. So I always ask. I remember that when Petra first came to Bracken Castle she felt very nervous. I offered to show her around to help her feel more at home.

THE LAND OF PYRAMIDS

This desert land is located south and east of Bracken. It takes thirty days to travel there by horse and boat.

The Land of Pyramids was built on the banks of the River Ar. The great pyramids and temples were built on the riverbanks more than two thousand years ago.

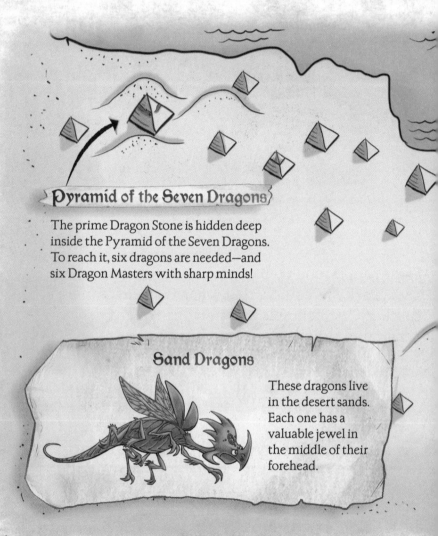

Pyramid of the Seven Dragons

The prime Dragon Stone is hidden deep inside the Pyramid of the Seven Dragons. To reach it, six dragons are needed—and six Dragon Masters with sharp minds!

Sand Dragons

These dragons live in the desert sands. Each one has a valuable jewel in the middle of their forehead.

Today, there are several good schools teaching science there. And because of the river, the Land of Pyramids became a great trading center. Books, fabrics, and spices find their way from this land to places all around the world.

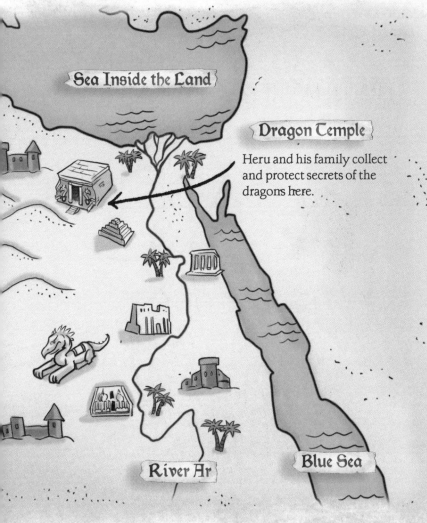

Sea Inside the Land

Dragon Temple

Heru and his family collect and protect secrets of the dragons here.

River Ar

Blue Sea

KEPRI THE SUN DRAGON

Every Sun Dragon is born with a Moon Dragon twin. Kepri's twin is named Wati.

DRAGON MASTER

Ana Gamal

Training Tip

Ana and Kepri practice making loops in the sky when Kepri flies.

POWERS

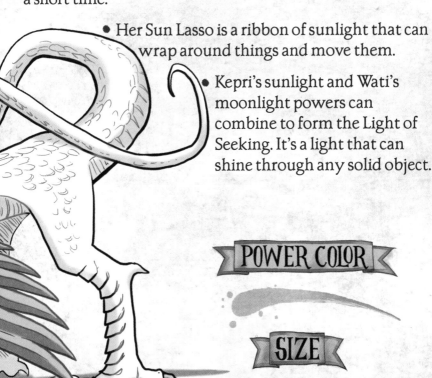

- Kepri is a very graceful, fast flyer.

- Her whole body can light up, just like the sun.

- From her mouth, she can shoot beams of golden sunlight and ribbons of sunlight in different colors.

- She can shoot out balls of light that will hang in the area for a short time.

- Her Sun Lasso is a ribbon of sunlight that can wrap around things and move them.

- Kepri's sunlight and Wati's moonlight powers can combine to form the Light of Seeking. It's a light that can shine through any solid object.

POWER COLOR

SIZE

LENGTH: 24 feet

WEIGHT: 2,600 pounds

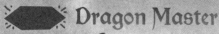 Dragon Master

HERU AL-TAREK

HOME

The Land of Pyramids

STRENGTHS

Heru spends most of his time reading ancient books and scrolls about dragons. Soon, he may know more about dragons than any wizard! He and Drake bonded when they searched for the Pyramid of the Seven Dragons together.

Dragon Secrets

Inside the Dragon Temple, there is a secret chamber filled with books and scrolls about dragons.

Heru comes from a long line of people who communicate with dragons. (In his land, they do not call these people Dragon Masters.) He lives with his parents, Sarah and Tarek, in the Dragon Temple. When he grows up, it will be his job to guard the ancient secrets of the dragons.

DRAGON

Wati the Moon Dragon

Dragon
WATI THE
MOON DRAGON

Wati is very similar to his twin sister, Kepri.
But where Kepri is light, Wati is dark.

SIZE

LENGTH: 24 feet

WEIGHT: 2,600 pounds

DRAGON MASTER

Heru al-Tarek

POWER COLOR

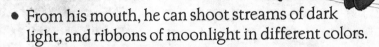

POWERS

- Wati is a very graceful, fast flyer.

- His whole body can glow with dark light, just like the moon.

- From his mouth, he can shoot streams of dark light, and ribbons of moonlight in different colors.

- He can shoot out balls of dark light that hang in the air.

  - His Moon Lasso is a ribbon of moonlight that can wrap around things and move them.

  - Wati's moonlight and Kepri's sunlight powers can combine to form the Light of Seeking. It's a light that can shine through any solid object.

Training Tip

Heru always trains Wati in the dark, when it is easiest to see his moon powers at work.

SUN DRAGONS & MOON DRAGONS

by Sarah and Tarek of the Dragon Temple

Sun Dragons and Moon Dragons come from the Land of Pyramids. They are always born as twins, from the same egg. The mother dragon can be either a Sun Dragon or a Moon Dragon.

Twin dragons have a special connection. They can communicate with each other over long distances. And they can cure each other of any illness. If the Moon Dragon is sick, the Sun Dragon can cure it with sunlight. If the Sun Dragon is sick, the Moon Dragon can cure it with moonlight.

The powers of each twin are equally strong. But a Sun Dragon's powers are strongest during the day, and a Moon Dragon's powers are strongest at night. They can also combine their powers for an extra-strong strike.

PETRA MARIS

HOME

Petra grew up in Helas, in the Southern Lands. She currently lives in Remus, where she studies with Dragon Master Tessa and Felix the wizard. But she returns home often.

STRENGTHS

Petra was afraid of being a Dragon Master at first, but she overcame her fears to save Drake and King Roland. She is a good researcher who can find answers to questions quickly. She communicates with a four-headed dragon, which is four times more difficult than communicating with one dragon! Like Heru, she loves to read about dragons. She and Heru write to each other and share notes.

Veggie Master

Petra does not eat meat. Her favorite food is hummus — a spread made of chickpeas, a sesame-seed paste, and garlic.

BACKGROUND

Petra's parents, Daria and Zale, work in the Great Library of Helas. Her great-great-great-great-uncle Cosmo was a dragon expert. Petra grew up among rows and rows of books from all over the world.

DRAGON

Zera the Poison Dragon

THE SOUTHERN LANDS

The Southern Lands are located southeast of Bracken. Helas, the land where Petra comes from, contains several busy cities. People from all over the world sail to Helas's coasts. Many people stay and live there. They bring their unique customs and food with them.

The Skav Empire

Pliska

Remus

Helas

Vitus

Helas is not far from the Land of Vitus and the city of Remus, where Petra now trains with her friend, Tessa.

-Griffith

The weather in the Southern Lands is usually much warmer than it is in Bracken. Many delicious vegetables grow there, as well as fruits so bright and colorful, they look like jewels.

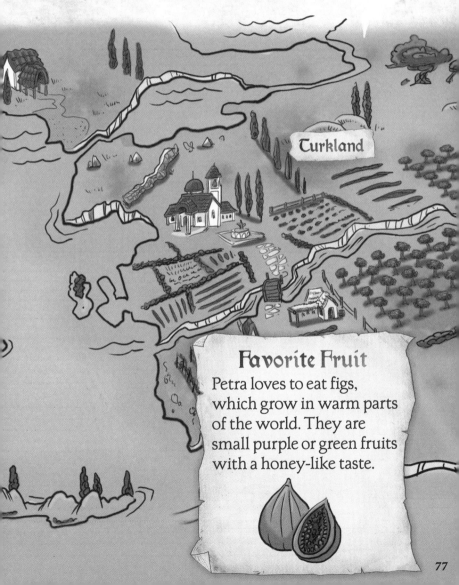

Turkland

Favorite Fruit

Petra loves to eat figs, which grow in warm parts of the world. They are small purple or green fruits with a honey-like taste.

THE GREAT LIBRARY OF HELAS

This library was built more than 1,000 years ago. It was the idea of Delia, a teacher in ancient Helas. She convinced Emperor Nikolas to construct it and fill it with books. Today this library holds more than 200,000 books and scrolls from around the world.

Reading Room

Visitors can take books from the shelves and read them here. The books are so rare that they are not usually allowed to be taken from the library.

Subject Groups

Books are grouped into thirty-six different subjects. Some of them include: history, medicine, mathematics, poetry, magic, and law.

Natural Light

A skylight keeps the reading room bright during the day.

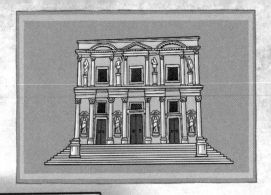

Statue of Delia

This statue watches over visitors.

Keeping Track

Library caretakers keep a record of each book's title, author, and subject.

ZERA THE
POISON DRAGON

Zera can appear frightening, with her four heads and sizzling poison attacks. But she is a gentle creature with unique healing powers.

Training Tip

When training a four-headed dragon, it is often easier to train one head at a time.

SIZE

LENGTH: 16 feet

WEIGHT: 8,000 pounds

POWER COLOR

- Zera can shoot different kinds of poison mist from her mouths. One poison can make humans and other creatures very ill if breathed in. Another can make anything it touches stop moving for a short period of time.

- Her four heads can sing in perfect harmony. This beautiful song can heal any creature harmed by her poison.

DRAGON MASTER

Petra Maris

Petra is experimenting with Zera to see what else her song can do. I have heard Zera sing a lullaby that can put anyone to sleep.

-Griffith

POISON DRAGONS

by Petra Maris

Poison Dragons, also known as Hydras, are very rare. They are found in the Southern Lands, and the last time somebody saw one was one hundred years ago. Zera may be the only one in the world.

No one knows how long a Poison Dragon lives for. I asked Zera how old she was, but even she is not sure. She said she has lived "for a very long time."

Every Poison Dragon has four heads. When I hear Zera's voice inside my head, I hear all four heads talking at once. So I think the four heads all think the same thing at the same time. But I need to spend more time with Zera and read more books to find out for sure.

Warning: Never touch the tail of a Poison Dragon! It makes them nervous. If you need to calm them down, gently pat or scratch one of their heads.

FELIX OF THE
ROLLING RIVER

MAGIC LEVEL

44

COLOR OF MAGIC

POWERS

Felix would rather read about the history of magic than perform magic. But he does have an excellent ability to create illusions using magical energy. During his battle with the evil wizard Marco, he created an energy horse that he rode across the arena.

BACKGROUND

Felix grew up on a farm on the Remus outskirts. He was thrilled when his magical ability appeared and he got to study at the Castle of the Wizards. When Petra took him to visit her parents in the Great Library of Helas, he disappeared in the book stacks for three days!

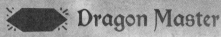 Dragon Master

CARLOS ALMA

 HOME

The Land of Aragon, where Carlos trains with Diego of the Sandy Shores.

STRENGTHS

I think Carlos may follow in Diego's footsteps and become a baby dragon expert himself one day!

-Griffith

Carlos took on a big challenge: to train a baby Lightning Dragon that is always shooting sparks! Patience is important when you are training a baby dragon, and Carlos has a lot of it. His grandmother taught him to be helpful and a hard worker.

BACKGROUND

When the Dragon Stone found Carlos, he was living with his grandmother, Nita, in a fishing village. These days, Nita, Carlos, Lalo, and Carlos's cousin, Val, all live in Diego's sprawling beach cottage.

DRAGON

Lalo the Lightning Dragon

THE LAND OF ARAGON

Aragon is a large coastal kingdom south of Bracken, and below the land of Gallia. Most of the people there live along the rocky coast. Aragon is known for having great fisherfolk, and skilled boat makers.

Vast Ocean

Sea Inside
the Land

Ursa

Queen Sofia

Aragon's ruler is known throughout the neighboring lands to be a peaceful and wise ruler. Queen Sofia is also known for her kindness. When a nest of baby dragons was discovered on top of her castle tower, she ordered that no harm should come to them. She immediately called for her royal wizard, Diego of the Sandy Shores.

Ursa Castle

Queen Sofia's castle, in the royal city of Ursa, overlooks the sea. Her guards all wear the color blue, and her royal symbol—a seashell.

Dragon
LALO THE
LIGHTNING DRAGON

Lalo is just a baby dragon right now, but his powers are very strong!

DRAGON MASTER

Carlos Alma

POWERS

- Lalo is made of energy, so he can pass through things that are solid, such as stone walls.

- He can fly with the speed of lightning.

- His wings can create sizzling lightning bolts and sparks.

SIZE

LENGTH: 12 feet

WEIGHT: He will not stay still long enough for Diego to weigh him. And because he is made of energy, it is possible that he doesn't have any real weight.

POWER COLOR

Training Tip

Baby dragons need lots of sleep! Carlos makes sure Lalo is well rested before any training session.

LIGHTNING DRAGONS

Every ten thousand years, energy from the prime Dragon Stone creates an egg. And out of that egg, one Lightning Dragon is born.

There is not much written about Lightning Dragons. Nobody knows how long they live. If the one born ten thousand years ago is still alive, nobody has seen it.

Diego and Carlos are studying Lalo to see what they can learn. They are also trying to figure out if Lightning Dragons and Thunder Dragons are related.

Lightning Dragons do not have parents like other dragons. Lalo was hatched from an energy egg and is the only one of his kind. He appears to be made of energy and does not have a solid body.

Thunder Dragons have parents and solid bodies. For that reason, Diego believes the two types of dragons are not related. (Look for more about Thunder Dragons later in this book.)

-Griffith

Wizard

DIEGO OF THE
SANDY SHORES

MAGIC LEVEL

51

COLOR OF MAGIC

POWERS

Diego has the power to transport himself anywhere in the world by snapping his fingers. He is a very good potion maker. Diego also has the magical ability to communicate with animals.

Flying Friend

One of Diego's animal friends is Bob, a seagull. He helps out when Diego asks him to.

Diego was born in the Land of Aragon. He attended the Castle of the Wizards, where he and Griffith became good friends. When he graduated, he was chosen to assist a wizard named Leda of the Raging River.

Leda had discovered a nest of baby Fire Dragons. There were too many for her to care for on her own. Diego helped her, and went on to become an expert in baby dragons.

Diego's Cottage

Today, Diego lives in a cottage by the ocean in Aragon. He can "poof" to Ursa Castle whenever Queen Sofia needs him. He also works with two Dragon Masters, Carlos and Val. He helps them train their baby dragons.

A Magical Alarm

The seashells hanging from the walls of Diego's cottage rattle when danger is near.

VAL ALMA

HOME

The Land of Aragon, where Val trains with Diego of the Sandy Shores.

STRENGTHS

Val is a quick learner who studied books about dragons, dreaming of becoming a Dragon Master one day. When Diego was called to help a nest of baby Invisible Dragons, Val knew just how to handle them.

I believe baby dragons are drawn to Val's kind heart. Being kind is one of the most important qualities a Dragon Master can have.

-Griffith

Val grew up in the northern part of Aragon, with their younger sister named Julia and a baby brother named Mateo. Val's parents, Marta and Juan, sent Val to live with Grandmother Nita when they got word that she was living alone. Today, Val and Nita live in Diego's cottage with Val's cousin, Carlos. But Val often visits with family back home.

DRAGON

Fig the Invisible Dragon

DOVE ISLAND

"Dove Island is one of the most dangerous places in all of my queendom!" Queen Sofia told the Dragon Masters. It is part of a chain of islands that lie south of Aragon, in the Vast Ocean. It is home to many creatures that have adapted to its difficult terrain and wild weather. But no humans live there.

High Peaks
You can try to climb these mountains, but it won't be easy to get up the uneven surface. And watch out for dangerous rock avalanches!

Rushing Rivers
It isn't easy to stay afloat in these swiftly moving waters.

Thick Forest
Between the cliffs and mountains is an overgrown jungle of trees and plants.

Hidden Cave
This cave leads to the rare and magical Dragon Tree.

Steep Cliffs
If you arrive on the rocky beach by boat, it's nearly impossible to scale up these high cliffs.

Only on Dove Island

The island gets its name from beautiful pink doves, which can only be found here.

There is only one Dragon Tree in the world, and it grows in the middle of a mountain on Dove Island. Invisible Dragons must eat its magical fruit when they are babies.

Dragon

FIG THE INVISIBLE DRAGON

Fig's parents, sisters, and brothers live on the grounds of Queen Sofia's castle. But Fig lives in Diego's cottage, where she trains with Val. Fig and Lalo the Lightning Dragon have become good friends.

Training Tip

Val ties a ribbon with a bell around Fig's tail. That way, if Fig turns invisible, Val can always find her!

DRAGON MASTER

Val Alma

POWER COLOR

SIZE

LENGTH: 49 inches

WEIGHT: 63 pounds

POWERS

- Fig can become invisible at will. Her other powers have not been discovered yet.

The Third Horn

Baby Invisible Dragons must eat fruit from the Dragon Tree on Dove Island before their third horn sprouts. If they don't, they will lose the ability to become invisible. When babies eat the fruit, their bodies glow with magical light from within.

Third Horn

Color Clues

All Invisible Dragons have scales that are a swirly mix of purple and blue-green. It can be hard to tell them apart. But Val quickly figured out that the fins around Fig's face are mostly blue-green, while Fig's siblings have mostly purple fins. Val, Diego and Carlos have found other ways to tell them apart. One has a solid green back, and another has only two bumps on her nose instead of three, like the others.

Carlos spent time taking care of Fig's siblings and helped name them after fruits, just like their sister: Berry, Kaki, Mango, and Kiwi.

-Diego

BABY DRAGONS

by Diego of the Sandy Shores

My good friend Griffith says I am an expert in baby dragons. I don't know about that! I have helped raise several baby dragons, but there is still so much to learn! Here is what I know . . .

Baby dragons hatch from eggs and are usually raised by their mother and father. They are born with their basic powers, but they do not know how to control them right away. With some dragons — such as Fire Dragons — this can be very dangerous!

In the wild, mother or father dragons keep their babies calm and show them how to use their powers as they grow. A baby dragon without a parent can harm itself or others. In that case, it is helpful to pair the baby dragon with a Dragon Master right away.

In my younger days, I assisted a wizard named Leda. She found a nest of three baby Fire Dragons with no parents in sight. While she searched for Dragon Masters for them, I cared for them. I learned that singing to baby dragons helps calm them. And for baby Fire Dragons, a splash in a cold pond works wonders!

When Zera sings, her voice calms Lalo.

-Griffith

Dragon Master

MINA OF THE FAR NORTH

HOME

Mina was born in the Far North Lands. She currently lives in the fortress of King Lars and Queen Sigrid, where she trains with Hulda of the Icy Plains.

Mina's Ax

Mina's ax might not be magical, but it is very practical. She can use it to chop wood and to break ice when fishing or climbing. She once used it to shatter a magical object to pieces!

STRENGTHS

Like many people of the Far North, Mina is strong in body and spirit. Mina traveled by herself for many days to save her kingdom. She does not give up easily, and she won't back down from a challenge. She bravely helped Drake and Caspar battle the dangerous wizard Astrid.

BACKGROUND

Mina's parents are Gyda and Erik, animal doctors who began learning how to care for dragons after Mina became a Dragon Master. She has a little brother named Fisk.

DRAGON

Frost the Ice Dragon

THE FAR NORTH LANDS

The Far North Lands are a group of four kingdoms just above Bracken. The kingdoms each have their own rulers.

King Lars and Queen Sigrid have been in power the longest. Their people are great sea voyagers.

King Albin's kingdom is the most remote. His people enjoy playing outdoor sports in the cold weather.

Kingdom of King Lars and Queen Sigrid

Land of Flowers

Princess Linnea

Frosty Gulf

Queendom of Queen Ev

The lands of Princess Linnea and Queen Eva have slightly longer summers than the others. Delicious vegetables and beautiful flowers grow here.

In much of these lands, winter lasts for six months out of the year. The people there have learned to live with ice and snow. They spend most of their time outdoors. They even invented a sport that involves pushing a stone across an icy pond with sticks.

Ice Fields

Kingdom of King Albin

River Joki

Dragon
FROST THE ICE DRAGON

This furry dragon has ice-cold powers but a very warm heart.

DRAGON MASTER

Mina of the Far North

When Zera the Poison Dragon sprayed poison mist at Frost, he froze all of the droplets in midair before they could harm him.

—Griffith

POWERS

- Frost has freezing-cold breath.

- He can blast his opponents with an icy chill.

- He can even trap them in a block of ice!

- He is a strong, fast flyer.

- Frost can create a Magic Ice Mirror that Mina can use to communicate with her wizard, Hulda.

SIZE

LENGTH: 20 feet

WEIGHT: 7,800 pounds

Training Tip

Like most Ice Dragons, Frost does not like warm weather. He is happiest training when it is below freezing outside.

POWER COLOR

ICE DRAGONS

Ice Dragons can be found in icy caves all over the Far North Lands. Each kingdom in the Far North Lands keeps an Ice Dragon around for protection.

The neck and belly of each Ice Dragon are covered in fur. This is not because the dragon needs to keep warm. The fur acts as a protective layer to keep the icy air inside the dragon cold.

Ice Dragons can stop all water attacks because they can freeze any liquid that is aimed at them. If you encounter something that has been frozen by an Ice Dragon, it is not easy to unfreeze it. Fire Dragons have the power needed to melt an Ice Dragon's blasts. There are no Fire Dragons that live in the Far North, so these dragons almost never meet. (Although Vulcan the Fire Dragon and Frost the Ice Dragon did meet once.)

Mina and Bo wanted to see what would happen if their dragons combined powers. Shu the Water Dragon created a curved stream of water. Then Frost froze it to form an ice bridge! It was quite amazing.   **-Griffith**

Wizard
HULDA OF THE
ICY PLAINS

MAGIC LEVEL

53

COLOR OF MAGIC

POWERS

Hulda is an expert in magic words, spells, and charms. When you say a spell to give an object magical powers, that object becomes charmed.

Charmed Object

Hulda charmed this spoon for the castle cook so that anything the cook makes with it will taste delicious!

Hulda and her sister, Astrid, both showed magical ability early. They studied together at the Castle of the Wizards. In the Far North, wizards are asked to return home to serve their king or queen when they turn eighteen. Hulda serves King Lars and Queen Sigrid. Astrid was sent to serve King Albin.

The rulers in the Far North always keep Ice Dragons, and the wizards there have been training Dragon Masters to work with these dragons for hundreds of years.

Hulda trains Mina, the Dragon Master of an Ice Dragon named Frost.

The Magic Ice Mirror

Hulda, Mina, and Frost worked together to create a way to communicate over long distances. First, Hulda charmed a Magic Mirror. Then Mina taught Frost how to create a mirror out of ice. Hulda used magic to link Frost's powers with her Magic Mirror. Now, Mina can reach Hulda whenever they are separated.

Dragon Master
OBI OKIRO

HOME

Obi lives in the Kingdom of Ifri.

STRENGTHS

Obi is very clever. At first, he thought he was not important enough to be Dayo's Dragon Master. But he has a strong connection to nature and knows about all of the animals in his land. It is his love of animals that helped him connect with Dayo. Obi became friends with Ana and Drake after they came to Ifri to find him.

BACKGROUND

Obi comes from a farming village, where he lives with his mother and father, Bisa and Kasim.

Exciting news — I found a young wizard named Ezinne who was ending her studies in Belerion to work with Obi! Now Obi has a wizard to help him as he learns to connect with Dayo.

-Griffith

DRAGON

Dayo the Rainbow Dragon

THE KINGDOM OF IFRI

The Kingdom of Ifri is a very large land that is south and west of the Land of Pyramids. It contains a desert, a mighty river, a waterfall, and great green fields.

The people of Ifri are known for their skills in math, medicine, and art.

Most people in Ifri live in villages or cities ruled by a group of the oldest residents. Every six years, all villagers vote on who will join this council of elders.

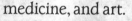

Council of Elders

Lion Mountains

Ozara Desert

Thunder Falls

Joliba River

The Marvelous Animals of Ifri

Warthog

This pig-like animal has pointy, curved tusks.

Elephants

These huge beasts are gentle and travel in groups.

Giraffe

This spotted creature has a long neck and eats the leaves of trees.

Apes

These furry animals are very intelligent.

Dragon
DAYO THE
RAINBOW DRAGON

Dayo might be the only dragon who lives in the Kingdom of Ifri. She has a very important power, and she is very, very old.

DRAGON MASTER

Obi Okiro

POWER COLOR

POWERS

- Dayo leaves her cave every spring and brings rain to the land.

- Although Dayo has no wings, she can fly and float in the sky.

- The stripes on Dayo's body are the colors of the rainbow. She looks like a rainbow when she flies across the sky.

SIZE

LENGTH: 48 feet

WEIGHT: 6,800 pounds

Training Tip

Dayo lives in her cave and is so old and powerful that she does not need to be trained by Obi. But they have a very strong connection, and they can call on each other for help at any time.

Wizard

EZINNE OF THE RUSHING WATERS

MAGIC LEVEL

39

COLOR OF MAGIC

POWERS

Ezinne has a special connection with animals. Some wizards, like Diego, can communicate with one or two types of animals. But Ezinne can talk to any animal she meets.

Furry Friend

Ezinne has made friends with a mongoose who is almost always by her side. She named him Agu, which means "tiger," because he is not afraid of anything.

Ezinne grew up on the banks of the Joliba River in Ifri. When she was five years old, her parents saw her talking to a bird. They sent her to Belerion to become a wizard.

When Griffith was searching for a wizard to work with Obi, Head Wizard Jayana said Ezinne would be perfect. Ezinne had the highest magic level in her graduating class.

Ezinne was happy to go back to Ifri to help Obi. She now lives in Obi's village. People come from miles away to meet the wizard who can talk to animals!

Learning About Dayo

Together, Ezinne and Obi are studying the Rainbow Dragon. They are watching Dayo and collecting stories from the elders. Obi writes everything down.

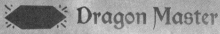

Dragon Master
JEAN ARCAND

HOME

Jean grew up and still lives in the Land of Gallia.

Jean's Silver Sword

Jean used silver from the Silver Dragon's lair to make this sword, as well as the gifts she gave to Drake and Bo.

DRAGON

Argent the Silver Dragon

STRENGTHS

Jean is a wonderful inventor! She creates tools that she uses to defend her castle, and things to make life easier and more fun for people. She is the guardian of the Silver Key, with her dragon.

Jean's Catapults

A catapult is a device that can launch objects into the air and send them flying very far. Jean's catapults have a heavy weight on one end and a basket of small rocks on the other end. When Jean cuts the rope, the weights drop and the rocks launch into the air.

BACKGROUND

Jean was raised by her mother, Amee, a master sword maker. Amee's workshop is a forge. There, she softens and hammers out metal in a fiery furnace.

JEAN'S WORKSHOP

Jean lives alone in the castle with Argent and has a lot of free time. To keep busy, she started making simple toys and useful gadgets using scraps of things she found around the castle. When her mother visits, she crafts strong metal pieces for Jean using the castle forge.

A Chair with Wheels

King Leon asked Jean for help after his daughter, Princess Colette, was thrown from her horse. Colette could no longer walk and wanted a way to get around on her own. Jean invented this wheelchair that moves when the user pushes the wheels. Colette loved it, and Jean now makes a wheelchair for anyone who needs one. Dragon Master Llew uses a wheelchair Jean made.

Making Plans

Jean's inventions all start with an idea she sketches on paper.

Easy Does It

This system carries items from the workshop to rooms all around the castle.

Catapult

This invention helps Jean protect the castle from invaders.

In Progress

Jean has tried to invent something that would help her fly like Argent. She has had no luck so far.

THE LAND OF GALLIA

Gallia is a small land not far from Bracken — just a short trip by boat across the Sea of Albion. It has been ruled by King Leon for almost fifty years.

Most of the people of Gallia are farmers. But many live in its largest city, Parisi. That city is known for its great food, poetry, and art.

King Leon

Officially, he's known as King Leon the Sage but his daughters — Princess Colette, Princess Maria, and Princess Claire — call him King Leon the Silly. Apparently, he likes to tell jokes that make him laugh, but make his daughters groan. They call these "father jokes." The king is beloved by the people of Gallia, probably because of his good nature.

The royal wizard of Gallia is my friend Sophie. She is an expert in magical rocks and gems.

—Griffith

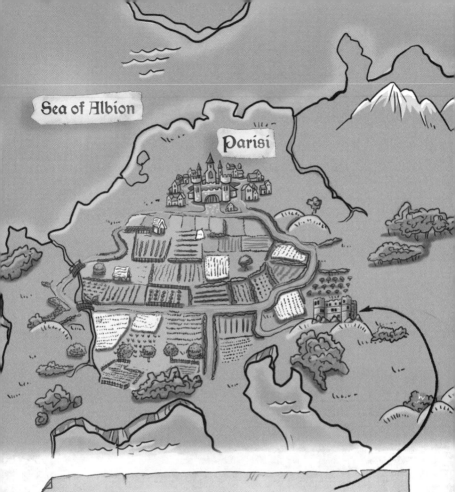

Sea of Albion

Parisi

Lair of the Silver Dragon

Jean Arcand does not live in the royal castle
of Gallia. She lives in a stone castle on a hill in
the countryside, far from the royal city. This
castle was built hundreds of years ago as a
home for Argent, the Silver Dragon, and is his
lair. A messenger delivers food and supplies
every two weeks.

Dragon

ARGENT THE SILVER DRAGON

Argent guards the Silver Key, one of two keys needed to control the powerful Earthquake Dragon.

DRAGON MASTER

Jean Arcand

POWER COLOR

SIZE

LENGTH: 36 feet

WEIGHT: 11,300 pounds

POWERS

- Argent can blast his enemies with his silver shine.

- When opponents attack, Argent can use his shiny wings to reflect their attack right back at them.

Training Tip

The only way for Argent to practice reflecting attacks is if he has another dragon to practice with. Jean may call on her friends for help with practicing this power — although Argent is already really great at it!

Along with the Silver Key, Argent guards all of King Leon's silver treasure.

-Griffith

Dragon Master

DARMA LI

Darma has always lived on the Island of Suvarna.

STRENGTHS

Darma is very in tune with the world around him. He may have learned some of these skills from the monks who raised him. He can sense what might happen in the near future. Because of his strong connection to the world around him, he always believes that everything will turn out all right. This keeps him calm in dangerous situations. He can also feel the energy of portals and magical objects and places.

Is Darma Magic?

Drake and Rori wondered this when they met Darma. Other Dragon Masters are not able to feel magical energy or sense what is about to happen in the future, like Darma can. Griffith thought Darma might be a young wizard, but Darma is not a wizard. He learned these skills in the temple where he was raised.

BACKGROUND

Darma lost his parents when he was a baby. He was raised in a temple by the monks who live there. A monk named Budi became his adoptive father.

DRAGON

Hema the Gold Dragon

THE ISLAND OF SUVARNA

Glory Peak

Ash Mountains

Cloud Mountains

Blue Fire Volcanoes

Great Sea

This island is very, very far from Bracken. It is even farther than the Kingdom of Caves. Suvarna is divided up into twelve kingdoms. Darma lives in the land ruled by King Wisnu the Brave.

It is very hot in Suvarna. The land is covered with green plants and colorful flowers. It is one of the few places in the world where you can find the Rainbow Tree — a tree with bark that grows in different-colored stripes, like a rainbow.

King Wisnu

The people there are great builders. They build palaces and temples that touch the sky.

Dragons are more common in Suvarna than in some other places. You can find Water Dragons there, and Flower Dragons connected to nature. But Hema the Gold Dragon is the most powerful dragon on the island.

Dragon
HEMA THE
GOLD DRAGON

Hema guards the Gold Key, one of two keys needed to control the powerful Earthquake Dragon.

DRAGON MASTER

Darma Li

POWER COLOR

SIZE

LENGTH: 34 feet

WEIGHT: 12,400 pounds

POWERS

- Hema can shoot beams of golden energy from her mouth. Those beams can blast her opponents, or wrap around them as though with a rope.

- She can change into any animal form she wants to.

Training Tip

Be careful not to ask Hema to transform into anything too small. Darma once asked Hema to turn into a flea, and then spent three hours trying to find her.

I would love to figure out how Hema's powers work. It is amazing that she can transform from a big dragon into a tiny mouse.

-Griffith

133

Dragon Mages
URI AND ZELDA OMEGA

HOME

Uri and Zelda have always lived on the Dragon Islands.

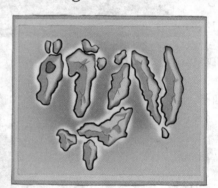

STRENGTHS

Uri and Zelda have one of the most difficult jobs a Dragon Master can have. They must protect the world from the powerful Earthquake Dragon, the Naga. The Naga is so powerful that the Dragon Stone chose two Dragon Masters, not one!

These twins are able to tap into the power of the Naga. This makes them Dragon Mages. It allows them to do things like float in the air and launch energy attacks at anyone who tries to control the Naga.

Uri and Zelda's mother, Chandra, and her twin brother, Ravi, were also Dragon Masters for the Naga.

The Twin Connection

The Dragon Stone chooses twins for the Naga every time, and they all come from the same family. The Naga always has two Dragon Masters, probably because more than one is needed to control the massive dragon.

DRAGON

The Naga, also known as the Earthquake Dragon

Most Dragon Masters do not become Dragon Mages until they are adults. I was surprised to learn that Uri and Zelda had become Dragon Mages at such a young age. Their strong minds — and the strong powers of the Naga — might explain why this has happened so fast.

-Griffith

THE DRAGON ISLANDS

This small group of islands sits in the middle of the ocean. There are sandy beaches, leafy jungles, and colorful flowers. But one island is inhabited only by the Naga's two Dragon Masters, and a small village of people who help take care of them.

The Temple of the Naga is located underground. It was created by wizards many years ago. They used magic to keep the Naga safe in his home, deep beneath the surface of the planet.

The wizards did their best to keep the Dragon Islands secret from the rest of the world. As a result, very few people have ever even visited there.

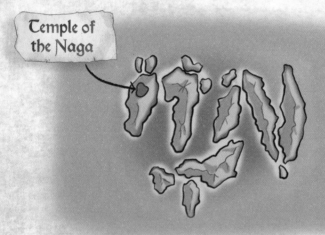

Temple of the Naga

The Naga is so large that his long body reaches many parts of the world. I have heard there might be a sort of "back door" to the Naga, as a way to reach the Naga in case anything ever happens to Dragon Island.

-Griffith

Inside the Temple

 A layer of Dragon Stone under the temple floor helps Uri and Zelda communicate with the Naga deep in the earth. The Dragon Masters can open a door to reveal the Naga's eye.

 There are also two keys that can open the door: a Silver Key and a Gold Key. The keys fit inside the eyes of the dragon statue above the door. Anyone who uses the keys to open the door can control the Naga's Dragon Masters. And whoever controls them can control the Naga!

Silver Key   Gold Key

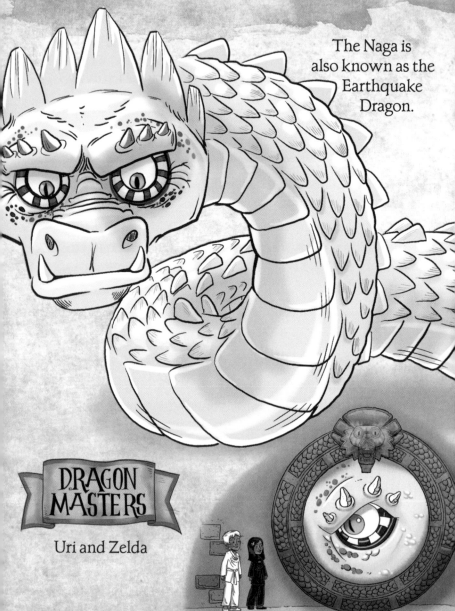

Dragon
THE NAGA

The Naga is also known as the Earthquake Dragon.

DRAGON MASTERS

Uri and Zelda

POWERS

- The Naga can cause earthquakes simply by turning his eye to a place. He uses the power of his mind to cause an earthquake there.

- The Naga can shoot powerful energy blasts from his eyes.

> The Naga may be the most powerful dragon in the world.
>
> *-Griffith*

POWER COLOR

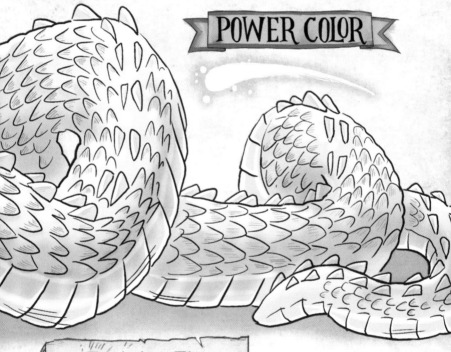

Training Tip

Uri and Zelda's main job is to keep the Naga calm and safe. When they train, they are learning how to channel the Naga's power and use it themselves to defend the temple.

SIZE

This dragon is so large that there is no way to measure him!

BREEN HANIGAN

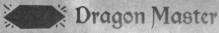

HOME

Breen lives in Inis Banba. She often visits her dragon, Fallyn, in the secret fairy world there.

STRENGTHS

Breen has a good sense of humor. And she is very clever. She also loves riddles and playing games, which is helpful when dealing with the fairy world.

A Friendly Monster

Blorp is a scary-looking ogre who is a friend of Breen's. Blorp is basically a good creature, but stay away from him when he's hungry!

BACKGROUND

Breen is the youngest of seven sisters. Her mother, Ina, is also the youngest of seven sisters, and is known for baking delicious cakes. Her father, Conall, is a beekeeper.

DRAGON

Fallyn the Spring Dragon

ÍNIS BANBA

Inis Banba is an island to the west of Albion. It is sometimes called the Green Island because of the rich green countryside there. Now we know that the land is so green because of Fallyn the Spring Dragon.

Vast Sea

Mave's Meadow

Inis Sea

Ancient Ocean

It is a good thing that Drake had Breen as his guide when he went there!

-Griffith

The Fairy World of Inis Banba

Fallyn lives underneath the green hills — in a secret fairy world. The fairy world looks almost like the world above it, but it is different. The sky is pink instead of blue. Colors look brighter. And all kinds of tricky magical fairy creatures live there, such as redcaps, pookas, and Hinky Pink.

The entrance to this world is a small hill known as the fairy mound. A wizard can usually get into the mound using magic. Breen's connection to her dragon means she can enter whenever she likes. Sometimes, fairies use the mound to escape the fairy world. When that happens, a fairy called a Royal Pixie Tricker is sent to bring them back.

Hinky Pink

Travelers get lost in Hinky Pink's magical fog.

Pooka

The Pooka can take any form, but likes being a horse the best.

Dragon
FALLYN THE
SPRING DRAGON

Fallyn may look like a cute dragon, but her power to make things grow is amazing!

DRAGON MASTER

Breen Hanigan

Legend says that Fallyn's Dragon Master must be a seventh daughter of a seventh daughter.

-Griffith

POWERS

- Fallyn can make plants of all kinds grow anywhere almost instantly.

- After winter is over, Fallyn brings spring to the land of Inis Banba.

POWER COLOR

SIZE

LENGTH: 23 feet

WEIGHT: 3,000 pounds

Training Tip

Breen is confident that Fallyn knows what she is doing. She prefers to sing songs and play games with Fallyn instead of training her.

NATURE DRAGONS

Some dragons are strongly connected to the seasons of nature in the land where they live.

Spring Dragons and Rainbow Dragons are Nature Dragons. You can usually find Spring Dragons in places that have a lot of plants and flowers. And Rainbow Dragons are very important to places that don't get enough water.

In the Western Lands, Tree Dragons change the color of the leaves of the forest. Wind Dragons bring winds to the high mountains of Ichu Mocco. In the Himala Mountains, there is a legend of a Winter Dragon that makes it snow. And different types of Flower Dragons can be found all over the world.

These are just a few of the Nature Dragons that have been reported. There are surely many more types to discover!

Tiny Moss Dragons live in the stone walls of the Castle of the Wizards. I saw a few of them when I was a student there, but they were too quick to catch!

-Griffith

147

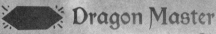

Dragon Master

LUKAS NOVAK

HOME

Lukas lives on a mountaintop in the land of Casgore. He stays in a cottage next to the tower that contains the Time Dragon's clock

STRENGTHS

As the Time Dragon's Dragon Master, Lukas has to learn how to operate and repair the magical clock that helps Maj use his powers. Lukas has a mechanical mind and is a fast learner. He is also very quick to tell jokes, and they often make his friends groan.

Most Dragon Masters train with a wizard, but not Lukas. He trains with a master clockmaker named Jelena.

—Griffith

BACKGROUND

Lukas was adopted by his dads, Gustav and Daniel. They say he gets his sense of humor from Gustav and is good at solving problems, like Daniel.

DRAGON

Maj the Time Dragon

THE LAND OF CASGORE

This land is known for its great, natural beauty — tall, snow-capped mountain peaks; sparkling lakes; and peaceful forests. Maj the Time Dragon has lived in Casgore for as long as anyone can remember. The first people of the land learned that if they cared for the Time Dragon, he would protect them in turn. Invaders have left Casgore alone, and the people there live peacefully and in harmony with nature.

The Lofty Mountains

Mirror Lake

Gothic

Queen Valentina

This queen has held the throne of Casgore for forty years. Her royal motto is "Live Well and Be Free," and her people call her "The Smiling One." She has vowed that anyone in the world who needs a safe place to live will be welcome in Casgore.

Casgore is not far from the land of Gothica. It is rumored that a Ghost Dragon lives in a castle there. **-Griffith**

Dragon
MAJ THE TIME DRAGON

Maj has some of the most impressive powers of any dragon. Where he comes from is unknown, but he once told Lukas that he is "as old as time itself."

DRAGON MASTER

Lukas Novak

POWERS

- When Maj shines a light on someone, he can see into their past to determine if they have a good heart.

- Maj can transport himself and others to any place in the world — and to any time in the past, present, or future.

Training Tip

Start slow! When Lukas first started working with Maj, he had Maj send him just five minutes into the past and then five minutes into the future.

POWER COLOR

SIZE

LENGTH: 30 feet

WEIGHT: 3,900 pounds

THE TIME DRAGON'S CLOCK

by Lukas Novak

Why shouldn't you share your secrets with a clock? Because time will tell! (Get it?)

But seriously, let's talk about Maj's amazing magical clock. The very first Dragon Master to connect with Maj was a clockmaker named Vid Oblak. Maj does not need the clock in order to use his powers. But Vid had the idea to create a clock that would make it easier for Maj to focus his powers on a specific place and time. With Vid's skills and a dash of wizard magic, he made the clock.

It will take me years of practice to learn everything there is to know about how this clock works. But it has three main faces. Once you know how to set the hands on the clock faces, you can make time fly!

Magical symbols let you set the place you want to visit.

The hands on this clock face let you set the month and day you want to visit.

This clock face lets you select the year you want to go to.

After the clock is set, Maj sits on top of it and uses his powers. Anyone who wants to transport must be touching the clock when that happens.

Thanks for reading my clock talk. I'm feeling a bit hungry. I guess Maj and I will go back four seconds. (Get it?)

Dragon Master

TESSA SILVAN

HOME

Tessa lives in Remus, one of the largest cities in the world.

Tessa's Staff

When Tessa is not riding Sono, she uses this staff to help her get around. She moves the staff in front of her, a little wider than her body, to make sure it's clear to take a step.

STRENGTHS

Tessa is confident and brave when faced with danger. She is blind and has a close connection with her dragon, Sono, who helps Tessa explore the world. Tessa and her friend Petra train their dragons together, with a wizard named Felix.

Tessa's parents, Livia and Titus, are musicians known for keeping the music of ancient Remus alive. Livia plays a stringed instrument called a kithara. Titus, who is blind like Tessa, plays the drums.

DRAGON

Sono the Sound Dragon

I am grateful to Tessa for keeping a cool head when her wizard, Felix, got into a magical battle with a dangerous wizard named Marco. I got turned into a duck trying to stop that battle! Thankfully, Tessa knew to bring me to the Castle of the Wizards to get help.

-Griffith

THE CITY OF REMUS

Remus is the biggest and most important city in the land of Vitus.

Hospital For the Infirm

Remus was the first city to build a place where sick people can come and be seen by doctors.

The Arena

Citizens gather here to watch sports competitions and magic demonstrations. They also come here to enjoy music and theater.

The Museum of Art

Remus is known for its great paintings and sculptures.

Diana Clara, the City Major

Every ten years, the residents of Remus vote on who they want to manage the city's affairs. The person who gets the most votes becomes the city major.

Diana Clara is the current city major. She was elected after the wizard battle damaged much of the city. She has been working hard to repair the damage and bring new businesses to Remus.

The Giant of Remus

For centuries, a huge statue of a soldier greeted visitors to Remus. It was destroyed during the great magical battle between wizards Marco and Felix. The people of Remus decided that the new statue should be an artist instead of a soldier.

City Walls

These strong walls have protected the city from invaders since ancient times.

Dragon
SONO THE
SOUND DRAGON

Sono and Tessa have a special relationship. Because Tessa is blind, Sono is often Tessa's guide as she moves through the world. Sono lets Tessa know what is happening in their surroundings. This helps Tessa avoid obstacles, interact with others, and explore the world around her.

Tessa Silvan

POWERS

- Sono and her rider can turn into sound waves and travel from one place to another at super speed.

- In her sound wave form, Sono can pass through solid things, such as walls.

- Sono can make powerful sound waves that break up rocks.

- She can make existing sounds louder or softer and control where they go.

Training Tip

When two dragons have powers that can work together, have some fun training both of them at once. Tessa and Petra are excited to find out if Sono's sound powers can make Zera's song powers even more powerful.

POWER COLOR

SIZE

LENGTH: 21 feet

WEIGHT: 2,800 pounds

Wizard

JAYANA OF THE FIVE PONDS

MAGIC LEVEL

64

COLOR OF MAGIC

POWERS

To become Head Wizard, Jayana had to master all forms of magic. She performs most magic with a simple wave of her hand or snap of her fingers. But her most impressive power might be keeping a school full of young wizards under control.

Jayana grew up in the middle of Sindhu, a land known for its large forests. She lived in a plain on top of a hill, noted for its five ponds of especially tasty water.

A visiting wizard noticed Jayana's talents when he saw the six-year-old girl make a mango float down into her hand from a high tree branch. She was sent to study at the Castle of the Wizards with Griffith and Diego.

After finishing her classes, Jayana was recruited as a Searcher. There are many stories about her adventures. Some say that on the way to locate a young wizard in Gothica, she battled a cave troll and won!

After her days as a Searcher, Jayana returned to the castle and became a teacher. When Head Wizard Flynn of the Steep Cliffs retired, Jayana competed in a series of magical trials with the other wizards who wanted the job. She got the top score and has been Head Wizard ever since.

A Searcher is a wizard who travels the world looking for magical children.

-Griffith

THE CASTLE OF THE WIZARDS

This is a school for young wizards, where children are sent when they show signs of being magical. The castle was built in a place called Belerion, where legend says the first wizards gathered in ancient times.

1 Advanced Wizard Hangout

2 Advanced Wizard Quarters

3 Advanced Wizard Classrooms

4 Mid-Wizard Quarters

5 Mid-Wizard Classrooms

6 Professors' Hall

7 Charm Workshop

8 Sky Observation Tower

9 Novice Classrooms
(For beginning wizards)

10 Novice Quarters

11 Library Tower

12 Main Entrance

13 Head Wizard's Office

14 Forbidden Objects
(Magically guarded to protect the objects from thieves)

15 Dining Hall

16 Infirmary

17 Potion Keep

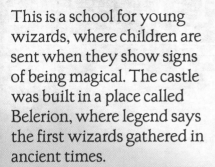

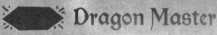 Dragon Master

CASPAR NAVIDI

HOME

Caspar grew up in a desert village in Navid. He lives in the Fortress of the Stone Dragon, not far from where he was born.

STRENGTHS

It was Caspar's quick thinking that stopped the evil wizard Astrid once and for all. He became good friends with Mina after Astrid turned them both into stone. When he visits Mina, he is sure to wear his warm coat. The Land of the Far North is a lot colder than the desert!

BACKGROUND

Caspar's father, Babak, is a shoemaker. His mother, Farah, takes care of his little sisters, Leila and Tara, and his baby brother, Ali. They all visit Caspar in the fortress.

DRAGON

Shaka the Stone Dragon

THE LAND OF NAVID

Navid is a land of large deserts, tall mountains, and rivers. Some of the deserts are so hot and dry that nothing can live there. But the Mustawi Desert is close to a river and has many underground springs. As a result, plants and animals thrive there.

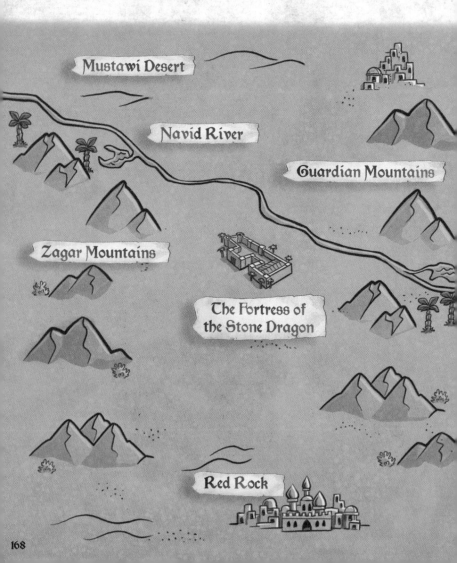

Mustawi Desert

Navid River

Guardian Mountains

Zagar Mountains

The Fortress of the Stone Dragon

Red Rock

Princess Daria

Before becoming ruler of Navid, Princess Daria studied at the university in the royal city of Red Rock. Then she spent two years as a soldier in the royal guard. She is now the chief command of the guard, which she uses to keep the peace in Navid — and to sometimes battle evil wizards.

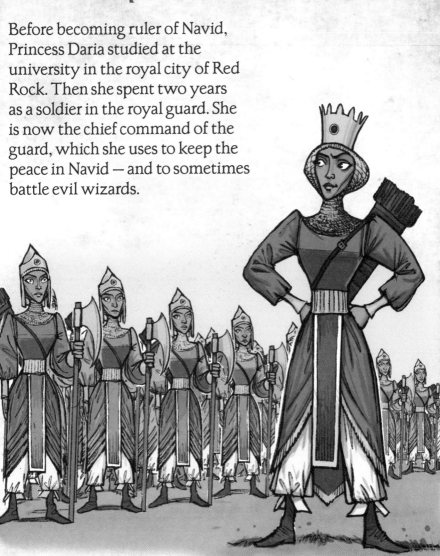

Dragon

SHAKA THE STONE DRAGON

This powerful dragon lives with her Dragon Master in a desert fortress. Together, they keep watch over a mysterious garden of giant bones.

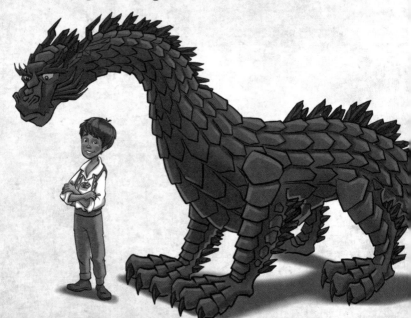

DRAGON MASTER

Caspar Hamad

SIZE

LENGTH: 29 feet

WEIGHT: 8,300 pounds

Training Tip

When Stone Dragons are first learning how to move boulders, they don't always have the best control. Make sure to keep a large distance between you and your dragon to stay safe.

POWERS

- Shaka can connect to anything made of stone and move it with her mind.

- She has amazing strength and can easily crush things using her extreme weight.

- Shaka has a Forbidden power. She can shoot gray beams from her eyes that turn living things into stone statues.

POWER COLOR

The connection that Stone Dragons have with rocks and boulders seems similar to the one Earth Dragons have. But Earth Dragons can move anything with their minds. Stone Dragons can only move objects made of stone.

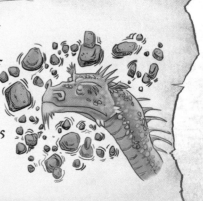

-Griffith

THE FORTRESS OF THE STONE DRAGON

This huge fortress sits in the Mustawi Desert. It was built to protect the Garden of the Beasts. These giant bones were discovered hundreds of years ago after a sandstorm uncovered them. Believing them to be very special and perhaps magical, King Hamid commanded the building of the fortress. Then he ordered a Stone Dragon and Dragon Master to stand watch.

The fortress is also used as a training camp for the royal guard. And it has served as a safe place for the Navid people in times of danger.

Ancient Painting
of the Beasts

Garden of the Beasts

Living Quarters for
Caspar and Shaka

The False Life Spell

Shaka and Caspar did their best to protect the Garden of the Beasts. But they couldn't stop Astrid from casting a spell that brought the giant bones of the beasts to life. The bones formed huge creatures — some bigger than dragons — that Astrid used as a ferocious fighting force.

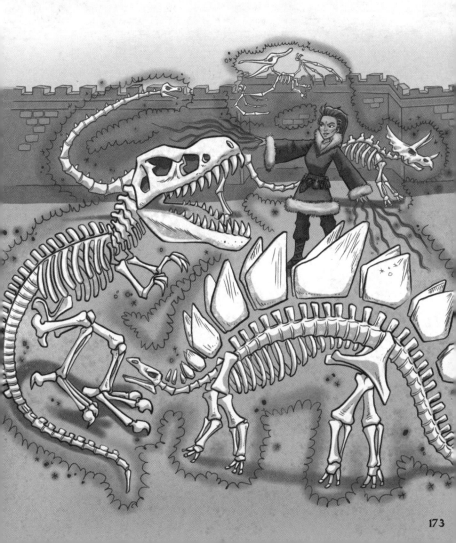

Wizard
ASTRID OF THE FROZEN RIVER

MAGIC LEVEL

55

COLOR OF MAGIC

The Red Crystal
Astrid once charmed a red crystal that allowed her to place people under her magical control.

POWERS

Astrid specializes in evil magic. She can create portals to travel from one place to another. She can shoot red magical energy from her fingertips and hands. And she has learned how to capture the powers of dragons and use them herself.

Astrid studied at the Castle of the Wizards with her sister, Hulda. After her training finished, she became the royal wizard of King Albin.

One day, Astrid's magic saved King Albin's kingdom from losing its crops, but King Albin took the credit. Angry, Astrid traveled the world learning evil magic.

When Astrid returned, she put his kingdom under a sleeping spell. She disappeared again and battled the evil wizard Maldred. She lost that battle, and Maldred trapped her in a magical wall for years.

Once free, she tried to cast a very dangerous spell. She failed and was turned into a statue. She remains in that form today in the Wizard's Council prison.

Astrid's Belt of Bottles

If a dragon attacks Astrid — say, with a fireball — Astrid can capture the attack in a magical bottle. Then she caps the bottle and hangs it from one of the loops on her belt. When she needs it, she can drink from the bottle and perform the fireball against a surprised opponent.

A wizard with stolen dragon powers?! I shudder to think what would happen if a wizard and a dragon could permanently combine their powers as one new creature. A Dragon Wizard? A Wizard Dragon? Either sounds terrifying!

-Griffith

Dragon Master
OPELI

HOME

Opeli lives on Manu, one of the islands of Noa in the Peaceful Ocean.

STRENGTHS

Opeli has a deep connection to nature. This is what helped her realize that there was something special about the dragon-shaped rock on her island. Ana believed her, and the two girls have been friends ever since. Opeli also has a wonderful imagination and enjoys singing.

The Ahi Stone

Opeli communicates with her dragon with the help of an Ahi Stone. Opeli noticed that her mother's Ahi Stone looked like a Dragon Stone. She thought it might allow her to connect with Ka. She was right!

BACKGROUND

Opeli's mother, Kalama, is a leader in their small village. An only child, Opeli often wanders off to enjoy the beauty of the island, making up songs and stories.

DRAGON

Ka the Lava Dragon

THE ISLANDS OF NOA

This group of islands is in a part of the world that stays warm all year long. Across the islands, you can find sandy beaches, volcanoes, colorful flowers, and fern forests. People travel by boat between the islands to trade goods and crops.

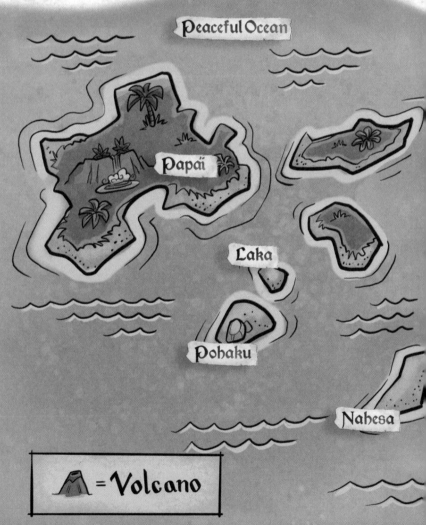

Peaceful Ocean

Papai

Laka

Pohaku

Nahesa

🌋 = Volcano

Leaders and Healers

These islands have no king or queen. Each village is led by one member, who is chosen by the villagers. Each leader works with healers — keepers of wisdom and magic — to manage and protect the village.

Hanu

Ohana

Manu

ʻiliʻili

 Dragon

KA THE LAVA DRAGON

Bubbling lava flows beneath Ka's scales, ready to explode whenever he gets angry.

 DRAGON MASTER

Opeli

POWERS

- Ka spews streams of boiling lava from his mouth.

- Before an extra-powerful lava attack, white smoke pours from Ka's nose and lightning streaks the sky. The same things can happen before a volcano erupts.

POWER COLOR

SIZE

LENGTH: 18 feet

WEIGHT: 4,900 pounds

An Ancient Legend

Lava Dragons are born in volcanoes and their bodies glow with fiery heat. The first humans who came to Noa were afraid of the Lava Dragons. Powerful healers used magic to send them back to the land. Ka took the form of a rock along the shore and stayed that way for hundreds of years. Then Opeli's connection with him — and Kepri's sunlight — broke the spell.

Dragon Master
MANAWA

HOME

Manawa lives on the
large island of Kapua.
It is located in the
Great Sea of Kiwa.

STRENGTHS

You need a big personality and
a strong will to connect with
a large Sea Dragon like Tani.
Manawa has both of those
things. He is also a great big
brother to his younger
sister, Pania.

Dragon Friend

Like Opeli, Manawa also
wears an Ahi Stone. But
in Kapua, he is called
a Dragon Friend, not a
Dragon Master.

Manawa lives with his family in the village closest to the shore. His parents are Mahuta and Epa. Besides his sister, Pania, he has an older brother named Kauri. The family works together with the other villagers to grow vegetables, fish, and hunt.

DRAGON

Tani the Sea Dragon

THE ISLAND OF KAPUA

Manawa lives on the eastern shore of North Kapua along the ocean. But Kapua is known more for its mountain ranges and green pastures than its beaches. Some of those mountains are volcanoes, which is where Manawa got his Ahi Stone.

Each village in Kapua has its own leader.

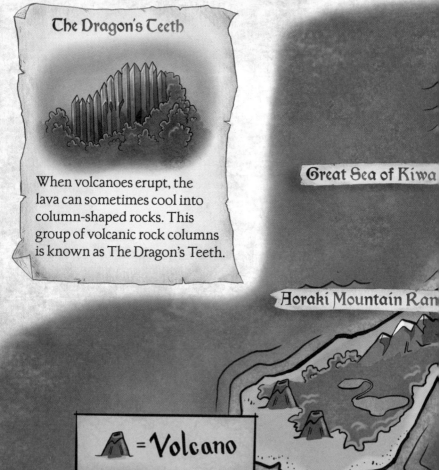

The Dragon's Teeth

When volcanoes erupt, the lava can sometimes cool into column-shaped rocks. This group of volcanic rock columns is known as The Dragon's Teeth.

Great Sea of Kiwa

Aoraki Mountain Ran

🌋 = Volcano

Peaceful Ocean

Noa and Kapua

Kapua is very far from the islands of Noa. But it is believed that long ago the people from those two lands all came from the same island. They journeyed across the waves to find new homes. Some settled in Noa, and others settled in Kapua.

Dragon
TANI THE SEA DRAGON

Tani lives in the Great Sea of Kiwa, off the shores of Kapua. She is twice as big as most other dragons — except for the Naga, of course. Tani is very strong and can kick up waves with a swish of her tail.

DRAGON FRIEND

Manawa

POWERS

- She can control ocean waves, causing them to rise and fall.

- Her greatest power is a *ngari nui* — a very, very big wave that causes destruction when it crashes on land. In some places, this is called a tidal wave.

Training Tip

Tani is difficult to work with when she's hungry. So Manawa waits to train with her until Tani has her morning feed of fish.

POWER COLOR

SIZE

LENGTH: 85 feet

WEIGHT: 12,000 pounds

AN ANCIENT RIVALRY

by Manawa

I was very surprised the day that Opeli and Ka the Lava Dragon arrived on the island. Tani the Sea Dragon was more than surprised to see Ka—she seemed angry. Then the dragons shared a story from a long, long time ago...

Many years ago, Lava Dragons and Sea Dragons lived together on the islands of Noa. Lava Dragons roamed the land, and Sea Dragons swam and splashed in the ocean.

Nobody is sure how the argument between the dragons first started. Some say it was a fight over territory. The Lava Dragons said the islands were theirs because they came from the volcanoes. The Sea Dragons said the islands were theirs because the ocean was created before the volcanoes.

The dragons' fight lasted for many years. The Sea Dragons tried to put out the heat of the Lava Dragons with great waves. The Lava Dragons sprayed lava on the Sea Dragons whenever they came on shore.

Finally Hahona, the oldest Sea Dragon, could take no more fighting. She convinced the other Sea Dragons to leave the waters around Noa. They swam far across the Peaceful Ocean and found new homes all over the Great Sea of Kiwa.

Dragon Master
QUILLA

HOME

Quilla is from Ichu Mocco, but she and her dragon had to leave to avoid capture by an evil queen.

STRENGTHS

Quilla is quick-thinking and smart. She knew how to keep evil Queen Amaru from using Wayra's powers to harm the people in her queendom. Quilla and Rori have a lot in common. They both love to fly fast, high in the sky on their dragons.

BACKGROUND

Quilla grew up in the large city of Ichu Mocco with her family. Her parents, Chasca and Illapa, are known for making beautiful pottery. Her brother, Colca, and her sister, Mayu, are both learning the trade. Quilla would have become a potter, too, if she had not been chosen to be a Dragon Master.

Wayra the Wind Dragon

ICHU MOCCO

Ruled by the city of Ichu Mocco, this queendom is in a mountain range. The people there call the ocean Mama Cocha, after the goddess who lives there.

Farmers work the land between the shore and the mountains, growing golden corn and potatoes with red and purple skins. The city is home to all kinds of crafters. Weavers create colorful designs in fabrics. Silver workers make beautiful jewelry. Wood carvers and potters make objects that are both useful and beautiful.

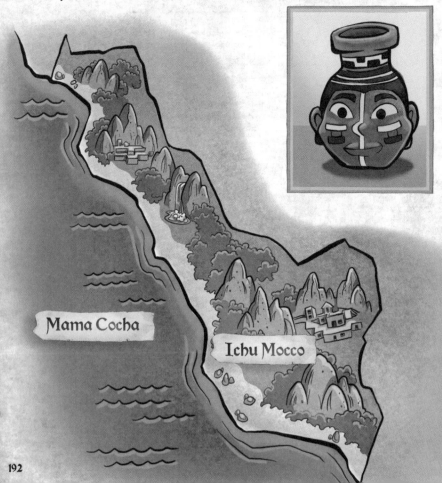

Mama Cocha

Ichu Mocco

Queen Amaru

Before Queen Amaru, Queen Inti ruled over a peaceful land. But Queen Amaru began training hundreds of new soldiers when she took power. And she captured Wayra to use as a weapon. Her people whisper that she plans to try to conquer neighboring lands. This is unusual because most rulers in the world took a vow against war fifteen years ago during the Great Peace Accord.

The people of Ichu Mocco do not want war. But most are afraid to stand up to this evil queen.

Dragon
WAYRA THE WIND DRAGON

A swift and graceful flyer, Wayra's powers can be as gentle as a breeze or as forceful as a hurricane.

DRAGON MASTER

Quilla

Training Tip

The best weather for training a Wind Dragon is a windy day, of course. They are experts at riding on the winds, and it seems to give them extra energy. But if a storm kicks up, avoid training. The combination of high winds and rain or snow can be too challenging for a Wind Dragon.

POWERS

- Wayra can communicate with any creature that flies, from bees to birds to butterflies.

- She can blow a mighty wind from her mouth that can knock any opponent off its feet or gently carry someone through the air.

- She can use her blasts of winds to create spinning tornadoes of sand or dirt.

Right now, Quilla and Wayra are safe from Queen Amaru. I have sent them to live with Oskar and Wildroot. I hope they will feel at home in the Lofty Mountains.

-Griffith

POWER COLOR

SIZE

LENGTH: 24 feet

WEIGHT: 1,000 pounds

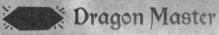

OSKAR LUDEKA

HOME

Oskar lives in the village of Stellburg, nestled on one of the Lofty Mountains. He lives in the dragon haven newly built by Lord and Lady Graystone. Quilla and Wayra the Wind Dragon live there, too.

STRENGTHS

Oskar has a sharp memory and knows all the legends of his land. He showed great bravery when he risked himself to save the Flower Dragons from a terrible monster. He learned a lot about being a Dragon Master from his friendship with Drake and Ana.

BACKGROUND

Oskar's mother, Nelle, is a baker. His father, Arnold, is a carpenter. They are the caretakers of Stellburg's new dragon haven.

DRAGON

Wildroot the Flower Dragon

Lord and Lady Graystone were so happy to hear about Wildroot, Stellburg's new dragon protector, that they paid for the building of the dragon haven. Brighteye, the forest sprite who looks after the Starflower Dragon tribe, sent her cousin, Whisper, to work with Oskar and Quilla. **-Griffith**

THE LOFTY MOUNTAINS

This mountain range is spread over many lands, from Casgore down to Aragon. Some of the highest peaks are in the region of Kinland. Oskar's village of Stellburg is located on one of these mountains, in an area ruled by Lord and Lady Graystone.

Lord and Lady Graystone

The Graystone family has ruled this area of the Lofty Mountains since the time of the Legendary Dragon of Stellburg.

The Legendary Dragon of Stellburg

Many mysterious and dangerous creatures live in the Lofty Mountains. A long time ago, a giant emerged from the Dark Forest and attacked Stellburg. A great winged dragon flew down from the mountaintop and drove the giant away. The people were so grateful to the dragon that they put up a statue in the town square. The dragon stayed and protected Stellburg for many years. One day, the dragon flew away and was never seen again.

THE LEGENDARY DRAGON OF STELLBURG

Stories about the Stellburg dragon say that she breathed fire. She does not look like a typical Fire Dragon, however. I wonder if she could be a combination of two or more dragon types?

-Griffith

WILDROOT THE FLOWER DRAGON

This little dragon is the leader of a large tribe of Flower Dragons in the Valley of Starflowers.

DRAGON MASTER

Oskar Ludeka

POWER COLOR

POWERS

- Wildroot and the rest of his tribe of Flower Dragons can release a mist that keeps humans from seeing them.

- They also have a special power called Bloom that can transform a werewolf back into a human.

SIZE

LENGTH: 14 inches

WEIGHT: 2 pounds

Wildroot is one of the smallest dragons I have ever seen. Moss Dragons are slightly smaller. And I have heard of dragons with insect-like powers that are so tiny they can fit on the tip of your finger.

I have read that Flower Dragons make flowers sprout wherever they walk. I have not seen Wildroot do this yet. I must ask Oskar about it!

-Griffith

FLOWER DRAGONS

No matter where you go in the world, you will find Flower Dragons. They may look different, but they all have many things in common:

- They all have green bodies.

- Sunlight gives Flower Dragons energy.

- Their powers are connected to the scents their petals make.

- On their head, wings, and tail they have petals that resemble the flowers they get nectar from.

- Flower nectar feeds the powers of all Flower Dragons.

Brighteye

It is very common for nature fairies to become Flower Dragon guardians. Brighteye is a wise forest sprite who looks out for the Flower Dragons of Stellburg. She can see visions of danger and warn the Flower Dragons before something bad happens.

Dragon Master
ARUNA

HOME

Aruna lives in the Temple of the Shadow Dragon in the land of Sindhu.

STRENGTHS

Aruna is not afraid to take big risks — like she did when she fed a magical seed to her dragon, hoping it would save the world. Also, her love for her brother, Darpan, is very strong. When she is not busy training her dragon, she loves to dance.

BACKGROUND

Aruna and her older brother, Darpan, were born in the city surrounding the Temple of the Shadow Dragon. Their mother, Lakshmi, is an artist. Her work appears in her home and on the walls of homes around the village. Their father, Hari, is a scholar who studies the dragons of Sindhu.

DRAGON

Chaya the Shadow Dragon

SINDHU

This very large land contains several different nations, each with its own ruler. The Temple of the Shadow Dragon is located in Tiru Nadu. Tiru Nadu is known for its beautiful temples. Many of them are hundreds of years old.

Tiru Nadu

Temple of the Shadow Dragon

Built in Tiru Nadu more than a hundred years ago, the temple i 208 feet tall. It is made of granite, a very hard stone.

King Vikram

The ruler of Tiru Nadu is known for his gentle spirit. He studies poetry and enjoys writing poems, too.

 Dragon

CHAYA THE SHADOW DRAGON

Chaya is a gentle dragon who uses his Shadow powers to keep people cool. After being cursed with evil magic, his powers became supercharged and he cast a shadow that could have kept the world in darkness forever.

DRAGON MASTER

Aruna

POWERS

- Chaya can create a shadow that streams from his nose. He can control where the shadow goes and even use it to grab things. The shadow can hide Chaya and Aruna from an opponent during a battle.

- Chaya can stream helpful shadow creatures from his mouth. (When he was cursed, these cute creatures turned evil!)

POWER COLOR

SIZE

LENGTH: 34 feet

WEIGHT: 5,800 pounds

Chaya is not an evil dragon. Eating the seed of the Balam flower made him that way. I have never known a dragon to do anything harmful on purpose, unless that dragon was under magical control.

-Griffith

MAGIC LEVEL

52 After returning from the Shadow Realm, Vanad discovered that his level had increased by four points.

COLOR OF MAGIC

POWERS

Vanad comes from a long line of wizards who can communicate with plants. He can use his powers to help them grow. Also, he is an expert on plants that wizards can use to create magical spells.

The Balam flower still grows in Vanad's garden. I know it will not produce a new see for one thousand year But I must speak to Vanad about how we protect the world fro its evil in the future.

—*Griffit*

Because Vanad's mother was a wizard, nobody was surprised when he showed magical ability as a child. At the Castle of the Wizards, he studied magical plants and also became fascinated with dragons.

When he returned to Sindhu, he asked to be assigned to the Temple of the Shadow Dragon. He trained one other Dragon Master before he became Aruna's teacher.

Vanad's Workshop and Garden

Vanad spends much of his time in the Temple of the Shadow Dragon, but his workshop is in a cottage not far from the temple. You'll recognize it when you see the sun, stars, and moons carved into the door. Inside, you'll find scrolls, books, bottles, potions, and magical tools.

The best part of Vanad's workshop is the garden he has out back, where he grows flowers native to Sindhu. He uses the flowers in his magical potions and spells. Anyone who has been in the garden says it smells even better than it looks.

THE BALAM SEED

by Vanad of the Flowering Garden

Legends say that the first Balam flower sprouted the day the first wizard in Sindhu was born, a long, long time ago. The flower grows quickly, but its petals stay closed for one thousand years. When the petals finally open, they reveal a red jewel. And inside that jewel is a magical seed.

The seed gives great power to the one who eats it. Every time a wizard uses magic, a Balam seed steals the power. The stolen power goes to the wizard who eats the seed. The seed will keep absorbing power until all wizards lose their magic, and one wizard has it all!

What happened to the person who ate that seed one thousand years ago? That legend has been lost. That wizard was my ancestor, and after a thousand years passed, it was my turn to eat the seed.

Aruna saved me from that seed. I saw how the power of the seed cursed her dragon, Chaya. I shudder to think what would have happened if I had eaten the seed myself!

jewel

seed

Chaya's Supercharged Powers

After Chaya ate
the Balam seed, he
started absorbing
wizards' magic. This
made his regular
dragon powers even
more powerful.

Cursed by the seed, Chaya could:

- Create a sky-shadow so big that it could cover
  the entire world in darkness.

- Use portals to transport throughout the sky-shadow.

- Flap his wings and send others into a spooky
  Shadow Realm.

- Send dangerous shadow phantoms
  streaming from his mouth.

After the Balam seed
was destroyed, wizards
around the world got
their powers back
instantly.

-Griffith

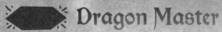

Dragon Master
RUNE JOHNSON

HOME

Rune lives on the largest of the Picland Islands, in a crystal castle overlooking the ocean.

Pony Master

Before he became a Dragon Master, Rune's favorite job on the farm was taking care of Picland ponies. These are the smallest horses in the world.

STRENGTHS

Rune is very good at solving puzzles. He's a great teacher, too. Rune is Deaf and communicates using his hands, not his voice. When he met Drake and Darma, he taught them several words in sign language.

BACKGROUND

Rune grew up on a farm with his parents, Breta and John. They are both Deaf, like Rune. Breta loves books, and she taught Rune to read. John loves games, and he makes puzzles out of wood for Rune.

DRAGON

Lysa the Light Dragon

THE PICLAND ISLANDS

This group of islands sits in the Far North Sea. It's a beautiful land, filled with green hills. The people there grow crops, herd sheep, and fish the ocean waters. In the winter, the days are very short. And in summer, there is light for as long as nineteen hours in a day. The islands have no king or queen, but each island is ruled by a lord or lady.

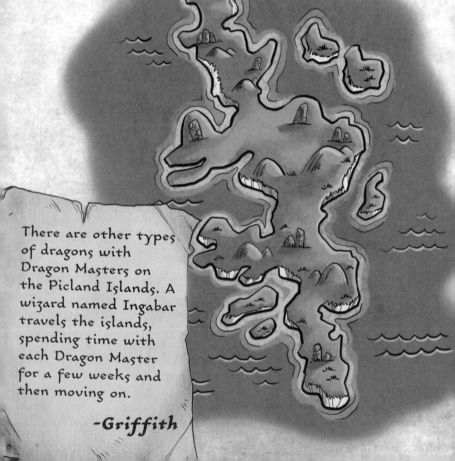

Crystal Castle

There are other types of dragons with Dragon Masters on the Picland Islands. A wizard named Ingabar travels the islands, spending time with each Dragon Master for a few weeks and then moving on.

-Griffith

The Labyrinth

The Light Dragon lives in a crystal castle near a magical maze. The maze holds the secret to summoning a Star Dragon. The secret is that the labyrinth protects the Star Flute.

The labyrinth appears to have been built by the ancient Picland people. Getting through the labyrinth isn't easy. First, you must pass the test of the Light Dragon. Then, you must figure out how to get through the maze, but it is full of traps and creatures that guard it. Magical creatures and challenging puzzles will try to stop you from reaching your goal. But here's a hint: You can't do it without friends!

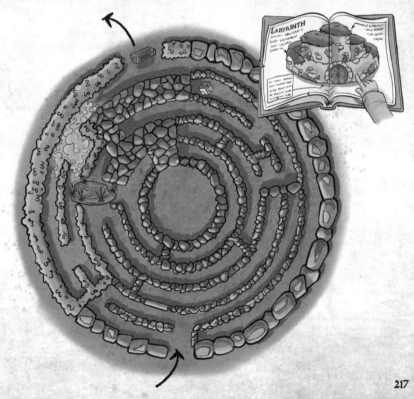

LYSA THE LIGHT DRAGON

There has always been a Light Dragon to guard the labyrinth on the Picland Islands. During the islands' long winter days, people travel to the crystal castle to be cheered by Lysa's light.

DRAGON MASTER

Rune Johnson

POWER COLOR

SIZE

LENGTH: 33 feet

WEIGHT: 2,800 pounds

POWERS

- If Lysa shines the Light of Truth on you, rainbow light will surround you, and you won't be able to tell a lie.

- She shoots bright white beams of light out of the symbol on her chest. This light was strong enough to push away part of the evil sky-shadow.

- It's impossible to get through the labyrinth without Lysa's light shining on some of the hidden clues there.

A Close Connection

Rune cannot hear, and Lysa can. But Rune and Lysa understand each other's thoughts. If Lysa hears a strange or dangerous noise, she can let Rune know using her thoughts.

Lysa is the only Light Dragon on the Picland Islands. But I suspect that Light Dragons can be found in other parts of the world.

-Griffith

MY LANGUAGE

by Rune Johnson

I was born Deaf. My parents have been communicating with me in sign language since I was born. Recently, I taught my friends Drake and Darma some words in sign language. I'd like to share those signs here.

When you talk in sign language, the main hand you use is the same as the one you write with. For me, that's my right hand.

Dragon

Put your hand in front of your mouth, with your palm down and your fingers forward. Then wiggle your fingers and move them forward, like flames coming from a dragon's mouth.

Follow Me

Make a fist with both hands and stick up your thumbs. Hold your left hand slightly higher than the right. Move both fists forward and to the left. Then point at your chest with the pointer finger on your right hand.

Danger

Hold your left hand in front of your chest, with your palm flat and elbow out. Make a fist with your right hand and stick your thumb up. Brush this fist against the left hand several times.

Thank You

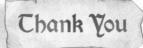

Put one hand flat in front of your mouth, with your palm facing you. Touch your fingertips to your lips. Then move your hand forward and a little bit down.

Friend

Curve the first fingers on both hands into "C" shapes. Then make two moves:

- Hook your right finger over your left.
- Hook your left finger over your right. It looks like two friends giving each other a hug!

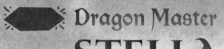

Dragon Master
STELLA OF THE SKY

HOME

Stella lives among the stars, in the dragon-shaped constellation known as Draco.

STRENGTHS

Stella's greatest strength is the love for her dragon, Nova. She took care of the baby Star Dragon after Nova hurt herself falling from the sky. Then Stella chose to live with Nova in the stars forever.

BACKGROUND

The legend of Stella is from ancient times, and there is not much that we know about her. According to the tale, she appealed to the goddess Harmonia to help her live with Nova in the stars. Harmonia played the magical Star Flute to grant Stella her wish. Then Harmonia hid the flute in the Picland Islands, so only those truly in need could summon Stella and the Star Dragon from the cosmos.

GODDESS OF MUSIC

> Stella is the only Dragon Master I know of who is also a magical being. She is very different from the other Dragon Masters, but she is also very like them. She is helpful and brave, and has a strong connection with her dragon.
>
> **-Griffith**

DRAGON

Nova the Star Dragon

THE DRACO CONSTELLATION

A constellation is a group of stars in the sky. When people gaze at the stars, they may think the stars form a shape, and they give that shape a name.

The constellation Draco looks like a dragon. Every three hundred years, a Star Dragon flies down from Draco and lands on Mount Sky. There, it lays an egg. When the egg hatches, the baby Star Dragon flies into the cosmos to join the others. They appear as twinkling stars in the night.

It is believed that every star in the constellation is a different Star Dragon. One of the "eyes" in this constellation is Nova the Star Dragon.

Song to Summon Nova and Stella

If you play "The Song of the Star Dragon" on the Star Flute while on Mount Sky, Stella and Nova will be summoned down from the cosmos.

If you can read music, try to play the song on a regular flute or recorder. You won't summon a Star Dragon, but you might like how it sounds.

Dragon

NOVA THE STAR DRAGON

This dragon can shine with the brilliant light of a star. She lives high up in the sky, in the Draco constellation, with her Dragon Master.

DRAGON MASTER

Stella of the Stars

POWER COLOR

POWERS

- Nova shoots star beams from her eyes.

- She can stream stardust from her mouth to surround and trap an opponent.

- When Nova whips her tail, it creates a rope made of starlight.

- Her Super Shine power creates an explosion of starlight. This light can destroy evil magic.

- Nova does not have wings, but she has the power to fly anywhere she wants to go.

SIZE

LENGTH: 39 feet

WEIGHT: Unknown

I know I have said that the Naga is the most powerful dragon on record. However, I wonder, is Nova even more powerful? Something tells me we have not yet seen all she can do.

-Griffith

LLEW REES

HOME

Llew lives in a village in Greenshire, which is part of the land of Cambria.

STRENGTHS

Llew is learning how to be a storyteller. He pays close attention to what's happening around him, and he's good at figuring out what might happen next when problems arise.

Llew's Wheelchair

Llew was just a baby when an illness left him unable to walk. His father was very excited when Dragon Master and inventor Jean Arcand made Llew a chair with metal wheels. Llew can move forward by placing both of his hands on the wheels of his wheelchair, pushing the wheels forward. He doesn't need anyone to push him.

Llew's father, Alan, is the Storykeeper of Greenshire. He keeps the past alive by sharing stories with everyone in the present. Llew's mother, Deryn, accompanies his stories by playing music on a stringed instrument called a crotta. She plays lullabies to help put Llew's baby sister, Elin, to sleep.

DRAGON

Belydor the Crystal Dragon

CAMBRIA

Griffith the wizard and Llew the Dragon Master are both from a county called Greenshire in the land of Cambria. The soil is excellent for farming. Most of the people there grow crops or raise cows and sheep. On the outskirts of Greenshire, you will find the Crystal Cave, where magical crystals grow — and where the Crystal Dragon was discovered.

Inis Sea

Albion

Greenshire

Crystal Cave

Ancient Ocean

King Owen the Clever

Twenty years ago, King Owen's two cousins, Emyr and Gareth, challenged him for the throne. They both gathered their armies to attack. But Owen convinced them to decide the matter by playing a board game instead of going to battle. Owen won the game, and he has ruled Cambria wisely ever since.

+ KING OWEN +

Dragon

BELYDOR THE CRYSTAL DRAGON

Belydor lives deep inside the Crystal Cave. For ages, he stayed hidden there. His powers are the source of magic for the crystals that grow in the cave.

DRAGON MASTER

Llew Rees

POWERS

- Belydor can shoot crystals from his body.

- The crystal points on his body can create a wall of protective light that shields him from attacks.

- He can shoot beams of crystal energy from his mouth. Those beams can hit you or trap you inside a giant crystal.

- Belydor can connect to crystals deep underground and call them up to the surface.

POWER COLOR

SIZE

LENGTH: 30 feet

WEIGHT: 7,400 pounds

Llew and Belydor met in a place that Llew calls the Dream World. Now that I know that Belydor has been to the Dream World, I wonder, could a Dream Dragon live there? I must ask Llew to tell me more about this strange new land.

-Griffith

THE CRYSTAL CAVE

The Crystal Cave is found on the outskirts of the village of Greenshire. Different kinds of crystals grow on each level of the cave.

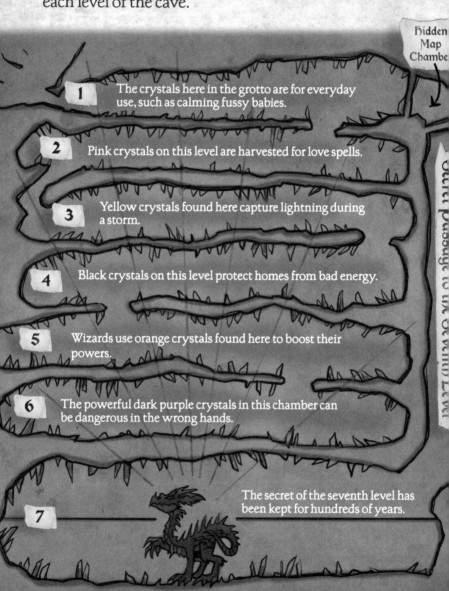

Hidden Map Chamber

Other passage to the seventh level

1 — The crystals here in the grotto are for everyday use, such as calming fussy babies.

2 — Pink crystals on this level are harvested for love spells.

3 — Yellow crystals found here capture lightning during a storm.

4 — Black crystals on this level protect homes from bad energy.

5 — Wizards use orange crystals found here to boost their powers.

6 — The powerful dark purple crystals in this chamber can be dangerous in the wrong hands.

7 — The secret of the seventh level has been kept for hundreds of years.

GEM DRAGONS

Crystal Dragons are part of a larger group of dragons known as Gem Dragons or Jewel Dragons. They are rare — just like the precious stones they're connected to.

Most gems can be found underground, and so can Gem Dragons. Known types of Gem Dragons include green Emerald Dragons and blue Sapphire Dragons. There have also been accounts of Ruby Dragons, Diamond Dragons, and Amethyst Dragons.

Because it is so rare to encounter a Gem Dragon, we know very little about them. But their powers are probably related to the gems. So a Diamond Dragon, for example, may have scales as hard as diamonds.

Ruby Dragon

Wizard

MORGAN OF THE GREEN HILLS

MAGIC LEVEL

40 As the official wizard guardian of the Crystal Cave, Morgan has not had the chance to sharpen his skills.

COLOR OF MAGIC

POWERS

Morgan has become an expert on the different crystals in the Crystal Cave. When he discovers a crystal he hasn't seen before, he experiments with it until he learns all about its magical powers.

BACKGROUND

Morgan is three years older than his cousin, Griffith. When a new wizard was needed to guard the Crystal Cave, Griffith was still in school. So Morgan was chosen. He has lived most of his life in his hut outside the cave. Villagers visit often to keep him company.

GERIK OF THE
MOUNTAIN PASS

MAGIC LEVEL

47

COLOR OF MAGIC

POWERS

Gerik is a master of spells of disguise.
He can make himself look like another
person, or he can camouflage himself to
blend into his surroundings.

BACKGROUND

Gerik and his younger sister, Inga, are both wizards from
the Lofty Mountains. Inga was always better at magic than
Gerik, and he hated being in his sister's shadow.

But Gerik loved to read. In a rare book, he discovered
the secret of the Crystal Dragon. He vowed to find a way to
control the Crystal Dragon and thus control the crystals, to
become more powerful than Ingrid.

His plan failed. The funny thing is, as Gerik carried out
his plot, his magic improved. He didn't need the crystals to
become a better wizard after all.

BECOMING A DRAGON MAGE

When a Dragon Master is first chosen
by the Dragon Stone, he or she begins
learning how to work with their dragon.
The more they train together, the stronger
their connection becomes.

After several years of training, a
connection between a Dragon Master and
dragon can become very strong. The Dragon Master
can learn how to tap into the powers of their dragon
and use them as their own. When this happens, a
Dragon Master becomes a Dragon Mage.

Eko, a former student of Griffith of the Green
Fields, is now a Dragon Mage. She can harness the
purple energy of her Thunder Dragon, Neru. Uri and
Zelda, the Dragon Masters of the Naga, also appear to
be Dragon Mages.

Dragon Mages will never be able to copy the full powers of their dragons. Eko cannot make thunder blasts the way that Neru can. But she can harness Neru's energy and turn it into power blasts, force fields, and energy leashes.

Not all Dragon Masters become Dragon Mages. But the best Dragon Masters will reach this level one day!

Dragon Mage
EKO IHARA

HOME

Eko grew up in Hayan, an island east of Emperor Song's empire. She lived in Bracken for a few years when she became Neru's Dragon Master. She now lives on an island in the Southern Ocean. But she returns to Bracken often to help Griffith train the Dragon Masters.

STRENGTHS

Eko is a Dragon Mage, so she can harness Neru's purple energy. She once used it like a whip to lasso Lalo the Lightning Dragon. Another time, she used Neru's powers to stop Worm from transporting.

Eko was the first Dragon Master trained by Griffith of the Green Fields. The Dragon Stone chose her after King Roland got his first dragon — Neru, a Thunder Dragon.

Eko loved Neru. But when the king began searching for more dragons to defend his castle, she became angry. She thought all dragons should be free — even though she had a strong connection with Neru.

She left the castle and took Neru with her. Over the years, her strong will and beliefs led her to do some harmful things. She attacked Bracken Castle. She kidnapped Lalo. She even teamed up with Maldred!

However, her friendship with Rori helped her to see things in a different light. Now, she is a friend to Griffith and the Dragon Masters.

DRAGON

Neru the Thunder Dragon

Rori reminds me of Eko, when Eko was the same age...

-Griffith

NERU THE THUNDER DRAGON

When you hear a loud boom in the sky, it may be thunder — or it may be Neru!

POWER COLOR

POWERS

- Neru can create a purple shield that protects him from attacks.

- His huge thunder booms shake the earth and can knock dragons out of the sky.

- He can make portals that allow him to travel to faraway places.

King Roland gave the emperor of Hayan a rare sapphire orb in exchange for Neru.

—Griffith

DRAGON MASTER

Eko Ihara

SIZE

LENGTH: 27 feet

WEIGHT: 4,800 pounds

Training Tip

If you are training a Thunder Dragon, make sure you have a very strong connection before you try creating portals. If the portal isn't done right, you could end up someplace you don't expect — and it might not be easy to get back!

WIZARDS' PRISON

Most wizards who do bad things make it up by doing good deeds under the watchful eye of the Head Wizard. But the most evil wizards are sent to Wizards' Prison, where they won't be able to cause magical harm to the world.

Wizards' Prison is located in a magical dimension. Nine wizards guard the doorway to this dimension, making sure nobody can get in or out.

The walls of the cube-shaped prison are made of Guardstone. It is impossible to use magic near Guardstone unless you have a wand with an Oppistone tip. Guards use these wands to get in and out of the prison.

The rooms inside the prison are very comfortable, because wizards believe that all people must be treated with dignity. Prisoners are given plenty of food and water, as well as musical instruments and books to keep them busy.

Only one wizard has ever escaped this prison: Maldred of the Red Hills. The Head Wizard has vowed that this will never happen again.

STRANGE AND DANGEROUS CREATURES

So far, we have discussed several evil humans who the Dragon Masters have faced. Power-hungry wizards and greedy rulers are always a danger to the world. However, Dragon Masters must be aware of the non-human creatures that can cause trouble.

Some creatures are downright dangerous, with sharp claws or troublesome powers. Others are well . . . just weird. And some that look dangerous may actually be friendly. On these pages, you will learn which creatures to look out for, so you can tell the difference!

-Griffith

Finsterbuns

These creatures from the Lofty Mountains look like rabbits with leathery wings, antlers, and sharp fangs. They won't harm humans, but they have a ferocious appetite for flowers.

Vasty the Ice Giant

Long ago, Ice Giants ruled the Far North Lands. Then the humans drove them out. One Ice Giant named Vasty became trapped in a tomb of ice. When he awoke, he froze the castle of King Lars and everyone in it! He's not giant anymore, though, thanks to Vulcan. The Fire Dragon's powers shrank Vasty into a tiny creature.

Kwaku the Spider

Kwaku is a giant spider from the Kingdom of Ifri. The people of Ifri tell stories about Kwaku. They say he likes to play tricks. He is not always dangerous. But if you see this giant spider, stay away!

The Redcaps

These magical little men march around the fairy world beneath Inis Banba. They may look cute, but if they find a human to play with, they will try to get that person to march behind them forever!

Beezel the Imp

Beezel is a tiny magical creature who used to be Maldred's pet. She can cast annoying spells that make you forget things or float in the air. She now lives on the Isle of Imps.

The Werewolf

Any human who eats a moonberry will turn into this monster when the moon is full. A werewolf is hairy, fierce, and hungry! Who knew that sweet little Flower Dragons would hold the key to stopping this monster?

Shadow Phantoms

After Chaya the Shadow Dragon ate the Balam seed, his helpful shadow creatures became evil. Swift and silent, their touch will turn you into a shadow.

Wood Sprites

If you are lost in the fairy world of Inis Banba, look for these winged forest fairies. You'll find them flying around the forest. They will help you — but maybe only if you answer a riddle first.

The Picland Beast

This creature lurks in murky ponds on the Picland Islands. To get past it, you will have to offer it something shiny and valuable. The beast will gobble it down but leave you alone.

The Griffin

Part lion, part eagle, this creature guards the temple on top of Mount Sky. Unless you know how to put it to sleep, you will find yourself on the wrong end of its claws.

Nasty Fish

Nobody knows their actual name, but they definitely are nasty! They swim in the moat surrounding the Dragon Tree on Dove Island. They have sharp teeth and they snap at anyone who tries to reach the tree. They're not evil — it's their nature.

IMAGES OF THE FUTURE?
by Griffith of the Green Fields

During the last full moon, my gazing ball began to glow brightly. Images projected from it. At first, I thought they were messages. But now I believe that they were scenes from the future. Let me show you.

This appears to be the Ghost Dragon in Gothica I have heard about! And that boy must be his Dragon Master. Will our Dragon Masters encounter them soon?

I believe I have seen this dragon in a book of ancient legends. I must do more research. She might be from a world different than our own...

Are those wizard symbols on this dragon's scales? What could this mean?

Another Earth Dragon! I'm sure Worm and Drake will be very happy to meet this dragon and her Dragon Master.

That dragon appears to be a Chaos Dragon from the land of Goryeo. If the Dragon Masters meet this dragon in the future, they might be in great danger!

Drake

Rori

Bo

Ana

Mina

Obi

Jean

Darma

Tessa

Caspar

Opeli

Manawa

Stella

Llew

Eko

Sandon

DRAGON MASTERS AND MAGES

Heru

Petra

Carlos

Val

Uri

Zelda

Breen

Lukas

Quilla

Oskar

Aruna

Rune

Kishar

Wolfgang

Nuna

Ji-Min

Never Forget!

If you have read this entire book, you are on your way to becoming a better Dragon Master. Maybe one day you will even be a Dragon Mage!

I will leave you with one last bit of advice. This is something I tell all of my Dragon Masters. To be a good Dragon Master, remember these three things:

1. <u>Kindness</u>: Be kind to your dragon, your fellow Dragon Masters, and everyone you meet in your travels.

2. <u>Curiosity</u>: Keep your eyes and your mind open so that you learn new things from the places you go and the people you meet.

3. <u>Teamwork</u>: When Dragon Masters work together, great things can happen!

Yours in magic,

Griffith of the Green Fields

TRACEY OF THE WEST lives in a cottage in the misty mountains. She wishes she had been a Dragon Master, but since she wasn't chosen by the Dragon Stone, she writes about dragons instead.

MATT LOVERIDGE is one of King Roland's royal illustrators. The king says, "His dragon drawings are the BEST!" He lives in the Rocky Mountains of the Far, Far, West with his wife and five children. His kids all hope to be Dragon Masters someday.

The sign language in this book is the same language used in the American Deaf community.

If you purchased this book without a cover, you should be aware that this book is stolen property. It was reported as "unsold and destroyed" to the publisher, and neither the author nor the publisher has received any payment for this "stripped book."

Text copyright © 2024 by Tracey West
Interior illustrations copyright © 2024 by Scholastic, Inc.

Photos © Shutterstock: cover gold (Allgusak), cover texture (Ensuper), cover banner (pedro alexandre teixeira), cover ornaments (PILart), interior background texture throughout (Lukasz Szwaj), interior header texture throughout (Sayan Puangkham).

All rights reserved. Published by Scholastic Inc., *Publishers since 1920.* SCHOLASTIC, BRANCHES, and associated logos are trademarks and/or registered trademarks of Scholastic Inc. The publisher does not have any control over and does not assume any responsibility for author or third-party websites or their content.

No part of this publication may be reproduced, stored in a retrieval system, or transmitted in any form or by any means, electronic, mechanical, photocopying, recording, or otherwise, without written permission of the publisher. For information regarding permission, write to Scholastic Inc., Attention: Permissions Department, 557 Broadway, New York, NY 10012.

This book is a work of fiction. Names, characters, places, and incidents are either the product of the author's imagination or are used fictitiously, and any resemblance to actual persons, living or dead, business establishments, events, or locales is entirely coincidental.

Library of Congress Cataloging-in-Publication Data Available
ISBN 978-1-339-02346-5 (hardcover) / 978-1-339-02345-8 (paperback)

10 9 8 7 6 5 4 3 2 1   24 25 26 27 28

Printed in India   197
First edition, August 2024
Illustrated by Matt Loveridge
Edited by Katie Carella
Book design by Sarah Dvojack